FESTIVAL OF DEATH

JUSTINIA WRIGHT PRIVATE INVESTIGATOR
MYSTERIES
BOOK 1

C W HAWES

CWH BOOKS

This one is for Jack, who believed in me
when I didn't believe in myself.
Rest in peace, old friend.

ENTER THE IMAGINATIVE WORLD OF
CW HAWES

Enter my world and you'll find that murder was never so good.

There's nothing like a good slow burn murder mystery. The quirky characters. The eccentric sleuth. The bumbling police detectives. The nefarious villain. And of course, the leisurely pacing until we reach the thrilling climax.

If you are new to the world of Tina and Harry Wright, then *Festival of Death* is an excellent entry point into the Justinia Wright Private Investigator Mystery series.

Tina and Harry are an homage to Nero Wolfe and Archie Goodwin. I so loved Rex Stout's world that I wanted to create one in the same style, but set in Minneapolis and the present day.

In my series, you'll discover the same type of exciting stories, eccentric and quirky characters, and wicked killers as Stout wrote about years ago.

So just click or tap the link below to enter my world of mystery and mayhem. You'll get a free copy of *Vampire House and Other Early Cases of Justinia Wright, PI* and you'll get my monthly email containing news and curated content. The game is afoot!

Yes, I want to enter the world of Tina and Harry Wright!

1

A BUCKEYE IS MISSING

THURSDAY MORNING, OCTOBER 4TH

I WILL NEVER UNDERSTAND why my sister, Justinia Wright, did not pursue a career in music. Take that gorgeous October morning, for instance. I was in the kitchen making breakfast, and she was in the music room playing Liszt's piano transcription of Beethoven's Sixth Symphony. The sound of the music filled the air, flowing through the rooms of the house and out the open windows to greet the Indian Summer.

The music ended, and she met me in the dining room where I had just finished setting the table.

"You're here," I said. "Good. I was about to call you."

She sat, while I retrieved our breakfast from the kitchen. Soft-boiled eggs, with toast sticks for dipping, sausage, a fruit salad, and tea.

On the dining room wall is a painting. The title is *After Shishkin's 'Brook in Birch Forest'* and the artist is my sister. She could've had a career in art, had she wanted, instead of music. But she passed by both options and accepted a job with the CIA.

After seven years, she quit, moved out to San Francisco,

and opened an art gallery, which she ran for two years. And when she tired of the art gallery, she bought this mansion and started her private detective agency.

She's been working as a private investigator for six years now, and, as near as I can tell, plans to keep at it until she retires. Where she got the money to buy her little mansion, which is worth more than a couple million, she won't say. It probably doesn't matter, unless she killed somebody for it.

Tina's not a morning person. Consequently, our conversations are minimalist to the extreme. Even the cats tend to leave her alone. She stared at her iPad, while I looked through the paper, and for at least the thousandth time said, "I don't know how you can stand having that newsprint on your hands and then touch your toast."

And for at least an equal number of times I replied, "There's an art in how you hold the paper."

She grunted. "What about the germs on the newspaper guy's hands?"

"Guess I'll die. Thanks for everything."

She smiled. Huh. She was in a good mood. The day should turn out just fine.

After breakfast, Tina went to the office. I put the dishes in the dishwasher, made tea, and joined her.

The room was already smoky, even with the windows open. The Muniemaker Long was sending forth a thin stream of smoke, which was making its way to the ceiling.

Tina was reading, and was oblivious to the fog. I turned on the fan to direct the smoke out and bring in some much needed fresh air. After all, we didn't want to suffocate our clients, who were due in forty-five minutes.

Two weeks ago, Mrs. Ralph P. Lowell telephoned from Dayton, Ohio for an appointment. She and her husband hoped to hire Tina to find their missing son. I'd made the appointment for ten this morning.

My sister hates missing person cases and would've turned down Mrs. Lowell's request, except I answered the phone. And when I take a call and the potential client wants a consultation with the great one, I go ahead and schedule a meeting. After all, you can't run a business or a household without cash. And when the owner of the business and head of the household insists on spending over fifteen thousand dollars for three bottles of vintage Terrantez madeira, her majordomo and Man Friday must see to it the cash continues to flow into the bank account. Hopefully in on amount greater than the outflow.

Tina was pissed, needless to say, when she found out. I pacified her with my research; namely, Lowell's upper six-figure annual income from his hardware store chain. If she takes the case, his wallet will be significantly lighter.

And she might not take it. She has refused before. More often than not, she sets an impossibly high fee and lets the potential client say no.

What she'd prefer to investigate are the cases where she's called in by the Minneapolis Police Department to consult. Those are usually murder investigations stumping the official investigators.

Too often when a person goes missing they want to disappear. Not always, though. Many young women are kidnapped and pressed into the sex trade. They for sure have no desire to be missing.

Precisely at ten, the doorbell rang. I got up from my desk and answered the door. Before me stood a man and a woman. He looked to be in his late sixties, and she, in her fifties.

The man spoke, "Good morning. I'm Ralph Lowell and this is my wife, Vera. We have a ten a.m. appointment with Ms. Wright." His voice was a rich baritone which complimented the camel-hair sport coat he was wearing, otherwise his appearance was rather ordinary. Mrs. Lowell, on the other hand, was anything but ordinary. One of those rare women time cannot touch. Like vintage madeira, time only improves their inherent quality. Her smile can still break hearts.

She was wearing a dark blue skirt and jacket and a white blouse. Her necklace was a strand of pearls and onyx. On her head was a small navy hat.

I replied, "Miss Wright, not Ms. As she would say, she is not a manuscript." I motioned for them to enter. After closing the door, I asked them to wait a moment in the foyer, and walked into the office.

"The Lowell's are here. He's doing his part for women's rights. He addressed you as Ms. Wright."

She wrinkled her nose. Tina distrusts any man who patronizes women. She sees nothing wrong with being a Miss. From her perspective, the prefix shows she is an available woman, and she sees nothing wrong in being available.

"He's not going to be…," she started.

"No. I don't think so."

"Good. Show them in."

I ushered our potential clients into the office. Ralph Lowell marched right in and took a seat on the chesterfield. For her part, Vera proceeded at a slower pace, observing the room as she moved. She sat next to her husband. Tina stood behind her desk while the Lowells entered. When they were seated, she sat. I took my place at my desk.

"I'm Justinia Wright, and you've met my brother and assistant, Harry. Would you care for tea?"

Lowell shook his head, but Vera accepted. I left, and made my way to the kitchen where I had a pot of tea on the warmer, in case our guests wanted a cuppa. I put pot, cups, milk, sugar, and lemon on a tray and took it into the office. I set the tray on the coffee table, poured a cup for Mrs. Lowell, one for Tina, and one for myself.

Mrs. Lowell said, "This room is a wonderful study in red, Miss Wright."

"Thank you. It is my favorite color."

Mrs. Lowell continued, "I paint and especially appreciate and enjoy monochromatic studies. You've achieved here an amazing variety of both color and texture. The varying lusters and hues of the cherry paneling, parquet, and furniture. The soft velvet of the curtains. The richness of this oxblood red leather sofa. And when combined with the contrast provided by the Oriental rugs and the dazzling painting in yellow. It is all quite simply intriguing."

"Thank you again. I'm glad it pleases you. I find this a wonderful place in which to work."

Mrs. Lowell sipped tea and smiled. "Not only are the eyes tantalized, but the palate as well. This tea is delicious. I've had nothing like it."

"It's a second flush Assam from the Orangajuli Estate. Harry can give you the address of the place where I get it, if you like."

"Thank you. I would like that very much," Mrs. Lowell said. She sipped tea, held the glass cup up to the light. "I notice even your tea has a reddish hue to it."

She and Tina laughed out loud. Lowell was fidgeting. He didn't seem to enjoy the chatter. Perhaps time is money, and this spending of time wasn't making him any money. Or perhaps he was one of those who are uncomfortable when not in control of and directing the situation.

Lowell spoke. "Miss Wright, we didn't come all this way for a tea party. We have important business to discuss and perhaps we should get to it."

Mrs. Lowell said, "I didn't know you were all that

concerned, Ralph. After all, it was my idea to hire Miss Wright in the first place when you were content to sit there while the police did nothing."

Lowell looked at his wife as if she were Benedict Arnold redivivus, then turned back to Tina, but she spoke first.

"Mr. Lowell, this is my office. I run my business as I see fit. Surely you cannot be in that much of a rush when your flight home departs at seven tonight. We may be here for several hours. Therefore, you might as well make yourself comfortable. If you don't care for tea, I can offer you sherry or madeira. I don't serve coffee. I also have Maker's Mark or Beefeaters, if you prefer."

At the mention of the time of his return flight, Lowell started. "How do you know when my flight home is?"

"I checked," Tina replied. "Didn't Harry tell you I would?"

"Yes, but..."

"Mr. Lowell, I run a business. Which means, as you are aware, I must make a profit to stay in business. Surely you understand?"

He nodded.

Tina continued, "If I accept a client, especially an out-of-town client, I want to make sure I get paid. Hence a brief background check is in order. In your case, we did a bit more than a brief check. I believe Harry explained over the phone, my fees are not cheap."

His countenance significantly brightened when he discovered it was about money. Apparently Lowell understands money. However, a frown settled on his face, and he asked, "Why more than a brief background check?"

Tina smiled, "I wanted to make sure about your income. I didn't realize the hardware business could be so lucrative."

He said, "Anything can be lucrative if you play your cards right. Since I'll probably be paying for it in the end, I'll try the madeira. I didn't think anyone drank the stuff. Thought only chefs used it."

"Au contraire," Tina replied. "Sweet, dry, or in the middle?"

"Dry."

I got up from my desk, stepped over to the cupboard, poured a glass of Sercial, and took it to Lowell. I left the decanter, too, in case he wanted a refill.

He took a sip. "Interesting stuff. Huh. Might even like it."

Tina smiled. "Let's get started. Shall we?"

The Lowells nodded their agreement.

"Mrs. Lowell, you told Harry your son was missing, and you wanted to hire me to find him."

"That's correct," she replied.

"The question needs to be asked," Tina continued, "does he want to be found? If not, you could be spending lots of money for nothing."

"Miss Wright, our son was traveling around the country trying to find himself, as they say."

"Nuts, Vera. He's a bum. Plain and simple."

"Now, Ralph, just because you don't approve of such things doesn't mean he's a bum. He's trying to find a purpose in life. Something, I guess, we didn't give him."

"That's a pile of crap and you know it."

"No, I don't, Ralph, no I don't." Her voice was still soft, but there was fire in it.

Their eyes locked for a few moments of silent combat. Then Ralph withdrew to study his glass of madeira and Vera focused on her hands, apparently deciding they needed some attention. They sat that way for several moments. Tina, with tented fingers touching her lips, simply observed.

I decided to play referee and, if nothing else, at least get them back to their respective corners. I've seen similar situations before and Tina will sit there with steepled fingers, not saying anything, letting the clients duke it out. Once an hour passed. At the end of which, when the conversation started up again, she named a retainer which was obviously ridiculous and the potential clients were no longer potential nor clients. I didn't want a repeat. I spoke, and Tina shot me a frown. "Mrs. Lowell, since you started, why don't you continue. Mr. Lowell, when your wife is finished, you can add anything she may have left out."

Mrs. Lowell looked at me and smiled. My heart melted. She turned to Tina and continued, "Edmund, our son, was traveling around the country. Once a month he would call me to tell me where he was, what he was doing, and assure me he was all right."

"He didn't speak to both of you?" Tina asked.

"No." Vera shot a look at Ralph capable of reigniting the Hundred Years War, but he was studying his glass of madeira and missed it. Peace in our time.

"He spoke only to you?"

"Yes. Edmund and Ralph were not speaking to each other. After college, Edmund, at Ralph's insistence, started working at the company's main office. He worked there a little over a year, then one night at dinner he announced he was quitting and was going to travel. Edmund said he needed time away from home. That he wanted to find his purpose in life."

"When was this?" Tina asked.

"Two years ago," Vera replied.

Tina nodded and Vera continued, "Ralph, of course, was furious. He was always furious with Edmund. Words were said, and Edmund stormed out of the house. Sometime the next day, Edmund came home, packed some things, wrote me a letter, and left. I'd been out shopping, and Ralph was at work. I found the letter when I returned home. As I said, that was two years ago. We haven't seen him since. He calls me every month. Except for the past three months. This month will be number four. Miss Wright, I'm afraid something terrible has happened to him and I'll never see my boy again."

Mrs. Lowell bit her lip to stop herself from crying. After a moment, Tina asked, "Did you bring the letter?"

"Yes. I thought perhaps you might want to see it, although I could repeat it by heart." Mrs. Lowell opened her purse and took out a white stationery envelope.

I got up and walked to Mrs. Lowell, took the envelope, and passed it on to Tina, who opened it, pulled out the letter, and read it. I waited by her desk. When finished, she handed the letter and envelope to me.

"Read it, Harry, and make a copy, please."

The letter was written in a bold, round hand. It read:

Dearest Mother,

I have packed a few things and am leaving. I have no idea where I'm going or when I'll return. But when I do come back, I will at least know myself and what I want to do with my life. What won't change is that I want nothing to do with Lowell Hardware. I will call you once a month (maybe more) to let you know where I am and how I'm doing.

Love you forever,
Edmund

I made a copy of the letter and the envelope and returned both to Mrs. Lowell.

Tina asked, "Did he ever call you more than once a month?"

"No, he didn't. I always hoped he would, but he didn't. Just once each month and never any day or days in particular."

"Thank you, Mrs. Lowell." Tina focused on Mister, who was still studying his glass of madeira. After a moment, she asked, "Mr. Lowell, why did your son want nothing to do with your company?"

He looked up and seemed rather surprised at the question. After a moment, he said, "I'm sure I can't tell you, Miss Wright. I have no idea what was going on in his mind. These young people get their heads filled with all kinds of crackpot ideas at college and then can't adjust to the real world."

"How was his performance at work?"

"Good enough. He was in training. I was having him work a variety of jobs so he would learn all the aspects of the business. It was my plan for him to succeed me as head of the company. I wanted him to learn the business inside and out."

Tina thought for a moment, then said, almost as if to herself, "It seems strange he would just up and leave, giving up money and prestige. To a man of his age, money's a powerful aphrodisiac with a lot of women. He could probably get most anything he wanted. His leaving makes little sense."

After a pause, she focused on Lowell and said, "Did he have any enemies at work? A bad experience?"

Lowell thought for a moment. "Not that I'm aware of. As far as I know, he was well liked."

"With your son out of the picture, what happens to the company?"

Lowell took a deep breath and exhaled. "Hopefully he'll come to his senses and take over, but if he doesn't I plan to sell the company. The Chief Operations Officer, Barry Osgood, and a couple board members are prospective buyers."

Tina thought for a minute. She opened the humidor and

looked at the cigars, sighed, and closed the lid. "Were you going to get rid of Mr. Osgood when Edmund completed his training?"

"Good heavens, no. My son would have become my assistant."

"How long has Mr. Osgood worked for your company?"

"I'd have to say about thirty years."

"How old is he?"

"Fifty-three."

Tina closed her eyes and leaned back in her chair. After a minute or two she leaned forward, opened her eyes, and asked Lowell, "Did Barry Osgood resent Edmund?"

"You're asking me if Barry…? I can't imagine… No, I don't—"

Mrs Lowell cut him off. "I don't think Barry Osgood liked Edmund. With Edmund out of the way, Barry was free to buy the company and become CEO and board chairman."

Lowell thought for a moment. "Barry has wanted to be CEO for a long time. But I don't recall him saying anything about Edmund."

"I do," Mrs. Lowell said, "I remember a company function a couple years ago, perhaps it was three, and you were grousing about Edmund not showing any interest in the company and Barry was right there with you in putting down kids and their communist teachers."

"That's possible, I suppose. I don't recall it. Anyway, Barry said nothing bad about the boy and that affirmed what I already knew. His heart wasn't in it."

Tina asked, "And it never occurred to you Barry Osgood might want to poison you about your son to further his own agenda?"

Lowell raised his eyebrows, and Vera's mouth fell open.

Tina continued, "Or perhaps even get him out of the way?"

"Now listen here, Miss Wright." Lowell was on his high horse. "Barry Osgood is a good man."

But Mrs. Lowell was saying, "Oh my God, that makes so much sense. How could we not see it?"

Tina had tossed a cherry bomb into their thinking, and they were going in opposite directions. She cut in, "Do either of you think Barry Osgood might resort to murder to get Edmund out of the way?"

Lowell was emphatic, "No way. That is ridiculous. Barry's a good man."

Mrs. Lowell was more thoughtful. She took a moment but finally said, "I don't think Barry would resort to murder, but he would poison the waters if he could."

Tina smiled at Mrs. Lowell. She turned to Mister. "What did you and your son argue about the night before he left?"

Lowell's exasperation showed plainly in his tone of voice. "That was two years ago. You can hardly expect me to remember words said in anger from that long ago."

"Perhaps not. How about you, Mrs. Lowell? Do you remember?"

"Not really. It was so much like all their other fights. Ralph always disapproved of Edmund's decisions. That night, I guess Edmund decided he wasn't going to put up with it anymore."

"When was the last time he called you?"

"June fifteenth. We talked for close to an hour. He said he was thinking about coming home."

"He was in Minneapolis then?"

"Yes. He'd arrived on the twelfth. He was staying in a shelter after being in the hospital for two days. He'd been beaten and robbed. He had no money and applied for welfare. When I heard that, I begged him to come home. He repeated he was thinking about it."

"When did you file the missing person report with the police?"

"August first. When Edmund didn't call in July, I knew something was wrong."

"Are you sure he wants to be found?"

"Miss Wright, as sure as I'm sitting here Edmund is in trouble. He had no intention of disappearing."

Tina sighed. "Very well. I think we're done for now. You brought the picture and completed the vital stats sheet I sent you?"

Mrs. Lowell nodded and took an envelope out of her handbag. I took it from her.

Tina said, "Good." She looked at Ralph Lowell. He looked up from his glass of madeira. "I will need a retainer of thirty thousand dollars."

My eyebrows went up and so did Lowell's. "Isn't that a bit much?" he said.

"He's your son," Tina replied.

"I know, but..." Lowell's protest was saturated with the dewdrops of resignation.

"Mr. Lowell, the case is old. Which usually means lots of digging. I'll probably have to hire more detectives. My hourly rate is three hundred dollars, charged in fifteen minute increments. Harry's is one hundred. We may have to grease palms, so to speak, to get people to give us information. Thirty thousand gives us room to work without having to ask for more right away."

A noble sounding speech. Pure business. And pure baloney. Tina didn't want the case. But she didn't want to say no. Perhaps the bank balance, perhaps Mrs. Lowell, were the inhibiting factors. So a thirty grand retainer and the hope Lowell would say "no" for her. But no such luck. Lowell looked at his wife and decided it was better to bleed in

Minneapolis. He wrote out a check, and I retrieved it from him.

Tina stood. Her personality is large enough. Now she looked like a giant. Her God-given six feet plus three-inch stiletto heels makes for quite a statement without saying anything. Ralph Lowell stood. He can look me in the eye and I stand at a mere five-ten. Not only did the poor devil have a lighter wallet, he now had to look up to the person who'd made it lighter.

Mrs. Lowell stood and asked, "How often can we expect a progress report?"

I replied, "I send a weekly update by email. When the case is completed, you will get a printed report."

They nodded.

"Anything else?" Tina asked.

They looked at each other. "No, I don't think so," Mrs. Lowell said.

"Then I wish you a good day," Tina said.

I showed them out and returned to the office. Tina had lit a cigar. I waved the smoke away.

"Go to hell, Harry."

"You are going to be a picnic to work with on this case."

"If he wasn't so afraid of catching hell from his wife, the thirty grand would have scared him off. Should've made it fifty."

"Right. And after the next purchase of vintage madeira, you declare bankruptcy. I thought a detective was supposed to detect."

"Shut up."

There we were. She sitting behind her cherrywood desk and I standing before it, glowering at each other through the fog of cigar smoke. Finally, I decided to act the older brother I am. I sat at my desk and asked, "Is it the case or Lowell or both?"

"You left out you," she said with a smirk. "Both. The case is old, which makes it a tough one to solve. Lowell is a pompous oink for one and for two I have a gut feeling there may be more to the issue between him and his son than either Mrs. Lowell is aware of or he wants known. Plus, this Osgood character. If there is something between Lowell and his kid, does it affect my approach to the case?"

"It might have nothing to do with the kid's disappearance. Or it might in fact give us a better understanding of why he left, which may have nothing to do with why he didn't call mom."

"No, it might not. The kid's been missing since at least July. The police have come up with nothing after two months, if they've even been looking. Now we're going to follow their footsteps down an ice cold trail and find the kid living in Blaine with a wife and two kids."

"I don't think he's been here long enough."

"Shit. The whole thing sucks."

"Look. You're just down because it looks hopeless. Of course the reason it looks hopeless is that it probably is hopeless. I mean the cops have been on it for two months now and nothing."

"To be honest, Harry, I'd bet those bottles of Terrantez they haven't done jack with this case. A transient out-of-towner goes missing. Big deal. Parents don't live here. Don't pay taxes here. What's a missing buckeye to them? They have no incentive to put any manpower on this."

"Which means we're essentially starting from scratch."

"You got it. But we should see what ground they've covered. After lunch, get hold of Cal. Hopefully, he can tell me what the boys in blue found. If, in fact, they found anything. Meanwhile, I have to think how best to scratch this itch I feel about Lowell. The kid just ups and leaves? Doesn't seem right and I can't help but think this itch might affect the case. Not to mention Osgood."

"You scratch away. I'll fix lunch."

She nodded, leaned back in her chair, and puffed on her cigar.

2

CAL SWENSON

THURSDAY AFTERNOON AND EVENING, OCTOBER 4TH

LIEUTENANT CAL SWENSON OF HOMICIDE, one of Tina's dearest friends and occasional lover, was at his desk when we came calling. In spite of his assurances he would be available, this wouldn't have been the first time we found him called away when we had an appointment. Standing at six-seven, he is the only person I know of who Tina literally looks up to. He came out to greet us, giving Tina a hug and a peck on the cheek and me a handshake. Which I prefer to a kiss, especially from Cal. He took us back to his office.

Once seated, he said, "How's the sexiest and most beautiful P.I. in Minneapolis? Maybe even the country?"

"What have I been telling you, Harry? Men. All they're interested in is a woman's brains. It's disgusting. For once I'd love it if a man loved me for my body instead of my head."

"Maybe if I saw you more often—"

"Or more of me more often."

"Well, that too." A huge smile spread across his face. "If I did see you more often, I'd get used to how gorgeous you look, and perhaps then I could appreciate those brains you claim are between your ears."

Tina leaned forward, placed her hands on his cheeks, and said, "Cal, you're just the sweetest hunk of Canadian Bacon I know." Then she kissed him.

"A complement like that doesn't come free of charge. What kind of jam are you in that Ol' Cal has to come to the rescue?"

"Shit, Swenson. You owe me so many favors I'm doing you a favor by cashing in on one so you don't have to count so high. If you can count at all, that is."

"What do you mean I owe you? If you remember—"

"Wait a minute, you two," I interrupted. "If you want to fight, get married. But I'd like a little information before you leave."

They looked at me for a moment and burst out laughing.

"Okay. Harry, what can I do for you?" Cal said.

"We need to know what, if anything, was discovered about Edmund Lowell. His parents filed a missing person report on him back in August."

"Hm. I'll see what I can find. Hang tight." He swung around to his computer. After a few moments, he said, "The case isn't being actively worked. He was reported as being homeless. Had been beaten up and was in the hospital. Apparently getting public assistance. John Berglund did some investigating. Here's his number." Cal wrote on a slip of paper and passed it to me. "Your subject seems to have disappeared in July from the local scene. If he was a drifter, he probably just moved on."

"His mother doesn't think so," Tina said. "Thinks he's in trouble."

Cal nodded. "Yeah. She called in to make the report. The kid stopped showing up at the shelters in July, it seems. Talk to Berglund. He might recall something he didn't bother to write down. These transients, though, come and go. No reason to think this one was any different."

"Except for his mother," Tina added.

"Yeah. Except for his mother."

"Thanks for your help, Cal," Tina said.

"Wait a minute, lady. I might be willing to do a favor for the Major here, cuz he's a hard working stiff. But from you I expect a little compensation."

"Compensation my ass. I already told you who has the credit balance around here on favors and it isn't you, Swenson." Tina stood up.

"Hey, Wright. You don't have to be so goddamn uppity. How about dinner?"

Tina looked down at him, And smiled, "When?"

"Tonight. Seven."

"Hm. Braxton's?"

"Sure. Why not?"

"Okay. See you there."

"Oh, no," Cal said. "I'll pick you up at seven."

"Really? Like a real date?"

"Like a real date."

She kissed the air. "You got a deal, lover boy."

"See ya."

"Bye." And she put a little swing in the porch on her way out.

In the tunnel, on the way to the parking ramp, I asked, "Want me to call this Berglund?"

"When we get home. I doubt he'll remember anything. I also want you to check out the homeless shelters. Even if Berglund checked, he probably didn't do anything more than go through the motions. Which means whatever he wrote in his report or happens to remember that he didn't write down isn't going to be of much help to us."

We got into Tina's Crossfire Roadster and made our way through the traffic to her pile on West Franklin Avenue. She parked in the driveway. Solstice, Tina's renter, had left her Land Rover out, making for cramped quarters.

"I'm going to have to talk to her again," Tina said. "She needs to put that behemoth in the garage."

"I'll let her know," I said.

"That's the problem. You're too soft with her.

"What do you mean?"

"Just what I said. You need to have a come to Jesus meeting with her and quit hoping she'll let you sleep with her."

"Wait just one minute."

"I mean really, Harry. You're twenty-seven years older than she is."

We walked into the house.

"I'm not interested in Solstice. Jeez."

"Yeah. Right. She's every man's wet dream."

"For God's sake."

Tina burst out laughing. "You're blushing, big brother."

"I have work to do."

I went to the office, and she followed me. I sat at my desk and she, hers. Manly, Tina's Manx, was sleeping on the sofa back. He opened his eyes, saw us, and closed them again. The moment Tina sat down, from who knows where, Isis showed up and jumped into her lap. Isis, one of those hairless Sphinx cats, is always looking for a warm lap. Prudy, a huge Maine Coon cat, waited until I sat down and then started rubbing up against my ankles.

I called Berglund, and he answered on the fourth ring. I told him who I was, how I got his number, and what I wanted. He had nothing to add and his response clearly indicated to me he had more important business at hand. I thanked him for his time and rang off.

"Berglund knows nothing," I said. Tina had lit a cigar and was pouring a glass of madeira.

She nodded and picked up the book she was reading.

I checked the internet for homeless shelters and found five in Minneapolis and one in St. Paul. Didn't seem like a lot to me, especially given what the nightly news seems to think is the number of homeless in Minneapolis. I've been homeless. I was lucky, though. I had my car to sleep in. And I was in a warm part of the country during the winter. To be homeless in the Twin Cities in winter must be hell. I also had Tina to take me in. That's how I came to be her majordomo, her Man Friday.

I said, "According to my count, there are five homeless shelters for men in the Minneapple and one in St. Paul. While you are out having fun, I will circulate with the photo of our missing person and hopefully find someone who's seen him."

Tina gave me the finger without looking up from her book. "I love you, too," I said.

I got up from my desk and went out to the kitchen. While making tea, I checked the fridge. Plenty of food on hand, but I didn't feel like eating any of it. With my tea made, I took the pot to the office. Tina wasn't there. Probably went upstairs to her room to change. I drank tea and looked at the list of shelters. Berglund had checked at St. Stephens and the Salvation Army, but not the others. Then again, had he really done so? Who knows? And if he did, it could very well be he'd checked with staff who hadn't worked on the night or nights Edmund Lowell had stayed there. Tina was right. This was beginning to look like we'd have to start from scratch on a case over three months old.

But if he's alive and isn't trying not to be found, we will probably find him. Only a matter of time. The most important piece of data we needed, we had: his legal name. We also had the second most important piece of data: an identifier to single out our Edmund Lowell from all the other Edmund Lowells.

Our identifier happened to be his birthdate. A Social Security number would have been better, but one takes what one can get. We also had a fairly recent picture to show people. Of course, the kid in the picture was clean shaven and the Edmund Lowell who visited Minneapolis might have been a woolly bear.

With that in mind, I fired up the scanner, scanned Edmund's picture into the computer, and began playing with Photoshop to give Eddy boy long hair and a beard. I'm no artist, so my attempt was on the crude side, but hopefully it would help jog people's memories if in fact he had a beard and long hair.

In the middle of my artistic endeavor, Tina showed up. She took one look and suggested perhaps she should do the drawing. I thanked her for her support.

"Suit yourself, Harry. I was only trying to help."

"Thanks. If I get people telling me no yetis have been by recently, you can try your magic. And you are really going all out, aren't you?"

"What do you mean?"

"Your outfit."

"Think Cal will like it?"

"Think? What's there not to like?" She was wearing an emerald green dress, just tight fitting enough to show all the delicious curves a man likes to observe. The neckline plunged to reveal an enticing amount of cleavage without giving away the store. She wore emerald green high heels and sheer nylons. A simple necklace of small ruby stones and a bracelet of gold and ruby completed her outfit.

"Thanks, Harry. Good luck. Please be careful."

"Thanks. I will. Enjoy your evening."

"I will. Love ya. Cal should be here. He texted me."

"Okay. Love you too."

And she was gone. I finished my retouched photo and printed several copies. Now to see what I could find. I grabbed my hat and coat and got into my car. First stop, though, was White Castle for a bite of supper. Cheese sliders and fries. What could be better?

With supper under my belt, I made for the Harbor Light Center and met with Envoy Clarice Broadman. I showed her the pictures, but she hadn't seen our missing person.

"If you leave the pictures and your card, I'll circulate them among the staff," she told me.

I did so and moved on, but got the same response at each shelter I visited. However, at St. Stephens, one of the staffers mentioned I might want to talk to Brother Leonard.

"Who's Brother Leonard?" I asked.

"I don't think he's a real brother, that is, a monk. I think he uses the title in the sense he's a brother to everyone in need. He shows up now and then to ask the men if they want work and a place to live. Usually one or two go with him. He must be pretty successful because we never see them back here. I think he has connections with a company out west."

I thanked him for the information and left him copies of the pictures and Tina's card, asking him to show them around. He said he would.

The clock told me the time was just after ten when I pushed open the door of home sweet home. I made tea and a sandwich and took them to the library. The hard salami and cheese, with lettuce, pickle, and mustard tasted good. I drank tea and considered I might have more luck showing the pictures to the men, well mostly men, staying at the shelters. I'd do that tomorrow.

In spite of the hope these places offer, I'm not sure they are all that successful. Successful in ending homelessness, that is. Last I heard, homelessness is on the rise while the number of employed homeless falls. Kind of difficult to hold down a job when you don't know where you're going to sleep when your work day is over.

People like "Brother" Leonard, who actually take a homeless person in and provide family-style support, are rare; but have better success in ending homelessness. Tina would never go for it, but she has plenty of unused space in this thirty room pile of hers. Plenty of space to give a few folks a temporary home. Her argument would be, "We're busy working to support this place and ourselves. What time do we have to devote to social work and do an efficient job of it?" And she would have a point.

The homeless often have severe problems, which cause barriers for them to secure long term employment and to manage their money effectively when they do have employment. Solving their problems is truly a twenty-four seven task, best handled by someone skilled and who can be with them twenty-four seven.

I sighed. Having been without a home for a time was rough. At least I have skills, know how to manage money, and ultimately had family who took me in and gave me a job. And that last is perhaps the secret to ending homelessness.

Tea and sandwich gone. I decided to hit the hay. Tina was still out and for all I knew might not show up until tomorrow morning. Just so long as she did. She had to decide how she wanted to tackle the Osgood angle and make a decision if she wanted to dig more into Lowell's history with his son.

3

NUNUS AND HOT DOGS
FRIDAY, OCTOBER 5TH

TINA SHOWED up at half-past ten. In the office, that is. I think she actually got home earlier because she was wearing her business attire instead of her evening attire.

"Did you get breakfast?" I asked, while she was getting settled at her desk.

"No. Would you be a dear?"

"Sure." I left the report and final bill I was typing to provide sustenance for my sister who had walked past the kitchen to get to the office. I am her Man Friday, and today is Friday.

Fifteen minutes later I was back with tea, toast, and a soft-boiled egg. "Here you are, m'lady." I put the tray on her desk and bowed.

"Thanks, Harry. You may return to whatever it was you were doing."

"Thank you, m'lady."

I returned to my desk. "Have fun last night?"

"I did. Thanks for asking." She conveyed a fork full of egg to her mouth, chewed, swallowed, dipped toast into the yolk, and did the same as with the egg. "You know, Harry, I really like Cal."

"I know you do."

"I just might marry him one of these days."

"Really?"

"Uh huh." There was just a touch of dreaminess to her answer.

"Must have been a really enjoyable evening."

"Oh, it was." And then the iPad, along with the food, stole her attention.

I finished the report and bill and got them ready for mailing.

When she'd finished eating, she put the iPad away and asked if my tour of the shelters had produced anything.

"Not really. Only talked with the staff and handed out pictures and our card. One of the staffers thought I might want to talk to a Brother Leonard who visits on occasion and offers men jobs. Tonight I want to talk to the men themselves and see if I get further."

"Okay. Eventually you'll want to check out this Brother Leonard."

"Made a note of it. Any ideas how you want to proceed?"

"I'm still not comfortable regarding Osgood, nor Lowell himself. But I'm not sure how best to make myself comfortable."

"What's the issue?"

"I have a hunch Lowell is the cause of his son's disappearance."

"How does that help us find the kid?"

"Don't know if it will help us or not. It might be that Lowell is the cause, but the information doesn't help us find Edmund. In which case, it is just information and has no usefulness for us. I haven't decided if it's worth pursuing or not. And the same goes for Osgood."

"You really suspect this Osgood of foul play?"

"Stranger things have happened. Edmund is gone. He's in unfamiliar territory. What better place to get rid of the competition and ensure your succession to the throne?"

"Okay. It's possible. Is it probable?"

"That, my dear brother, I don't know. Insufficient data."

"Seems to me, the kid disappeared here and we have to exhaust the avenues on our home turf before we go gallivanting all over the countryside."

"Anyone ever tell you that you are one conservative fellow?"

"Yeah, it's my middle name."

"You are probably right. Let's see what you come up with in your information gathering tonight and we'll go from there." And with that, she buried her nose in a book.

I got the distinct feeling she wasn't giving this case her full attention. And given she didn't want it, I'm probably right. I removed her tray to the kitchen and decided to make NuNus and Hot Dogs for lunch. Definitely not gourmet, but comfort food it is.

I was just about done when Tina walked into the kitchen. "What are you making?"

"NuNus and HotDogs."

"Are you serious?"

"Yes."

"*You* making noodles with hotdogs?"

"Yes. Moi."

"You feeling all right?"

"Yes. Why? Don't you want it?"

"Hell, yes, I want it. Haven't had that since we were kids.

God. This is a treat. Oh, by the way, Cal is going to come over tonight. Watch a movie."

"Really? Okay by me."

"You like Cal, don't you?"

"I do. Perfectly fine by me. Personally, I think you two should get married. You've had a long enough honeymoon."

She laughed. "Physician, heal thyself."

"Find me someone who loves me and won't dump me at the first pothole and I will."

"Okay, big brother, I'll see what I can cook up. Can she be a noodles and hotdogs kind of gal or does she have to be foie gras and champagne?"

"As long as she loves me, it doesn't matter."

"Okay. I'll see what I can do."

"Thanks, Sis. In the meantime, let's eat and find a missing person."

"Knew you'd work that in someway."

I took the food to the dining room, and Tina followed me. We sat down and dug in.

With fork partway to her mouth, she asked, "Do you think Stinky or Ed might get better results talking to the homeless guys?"

"Maybe. You'd rather have them than me?"

"No. Just who will get the best results."

"Okay. I'll call them and see if they're available."

We finished lunch, and I cleaned up the dishes, while Tina relocated to the music room and played Chopin. When the dishes and leftovers were dealt with, I went to the office and called Ed Hafner. He works for Bloodhound Detective Agency and occasionally freelances for Tina. He's a good solid detective. Not overly creative, but handles routine work well. He said he could work two shelters tonight. I emailed the pictures to him.

Why Stinky Johnson is nicknamed "Stinky", I don't know. He's a decent detective. Especially good in the poorer areas of the city. He's meticulously clean and well-dressed, and maybe that's why he's called "Stinky". He has the bad habit of once or twice a year going on a bender. Only he doesn't use booze, he drinks vanilla or almond extract. At forty percent alcohol, you can get buzzed rather quickly. Stinky was available and would circulate the pictures through the other shelters for us. I emailed the pictures to him.

That essentially left me free tonight. I decided to go out to eat, take in a movie, and then play it by ear. I'd rather not be around if Cal was coming over. Although with thirty rooms in Tina's pile there are plenty of places to get out of two horny people's way.

The phone rang and I answered, "Wright Investigations."

"Hey, Major."

"Hi, Cal. You coming over tonight?"

"Yeah. Tell Tina I'll be there around seven, will you?"

"Sure."

"Great. Thanks. Catch you later." He ended the call.

I got up and walked to the music room. Tina had moved from Chopin to Vaughan Williams. I conveyed Cal's message. She thanked me and I told her I was going out.

"You can watch a movie with us," she said.

"A car doesn't need a fifth wheel."

"Suit yourself, but you are welcome to join us."

"Thanks. Perhaps another time."

I returned to the office and looked over the information we'd gotten from the Lowells. One thing was missing: a list of places from which Edmund had called home. I shot an email to Mrs. Lowell asking if she could provide the information. Never know, it might be helpful. In the meantime, I looked at what we had.

On Tuesday, June 12th, Edmund Lowell arrives in Minneapolis. He's beaten and robbed and ends up in the hospital. Spends Wednesday and Thursday in the hospital. On Friday, June 15th, he applies for welfare and phones home. That's the last contact between Edmund and his mother. But certainly not the last time he's seen in Minneapolis. That was apparently sometime in July. Or was it? Could it be he left Friday night? Who knows? Did he take the bus to Milwaukee? Or did he hitchhike somewhere? Or is he actually still here?

I turned the information over in my mind. At this point, there was no proof Edmund had stayed in Minneapolis. Only Mrs. Lowell's gut feeling. Not a lot to go on, really. If Ed or Stinky didn't come up with something, then I was of the opinion we should call it quits. Looking for a homeless transient is on par with looking for a needle in a haystack and you don't know where the haystack is.

Mrs. Lowell was serious. I checked my email, and she'd sent a list. I printed the email so I could write notes on it. She'd noted date, time, and place of her son's calls. She even included notes of what they talked about. Those notes might come in handy later. But for now, I just wanted to look at his movements.

He was in Nashville when he made the first call home, which was two years ago this past August.

September and October it looked like he was in Alabama. The November call was from Galveston, and the December call was from San Diego on Christmas day.

After that, the calls came from all over California, until a year ago July when he showed up in Oregon. September he was in Seattle; October, Salt Lake City; November, Las Vegas; and December, back in San Diego.

Starting March of this year, there was a definite move to the east. Calls came from Roswell, New Mexico in April; Des Moines, Iowa in May; and Minneapolis in June.

I sat back in my chair and pondered the data. Most of his time was spent in California. Which makes sense. It's warmer there than, say, the rest of the country. But the data clearly indicated he was heading back east starting in March of this year. Maybe he was tired. Maybe he did in fact want to go home.

I put the sheet of paper down and thought of another homecoming a number of years ago. The fifth of May I knocked on Tina's door and asked if she could put me up for a few nights. I've been here ever since. Tina's not the type to cry. She keeps her emotions under control. I suppose her spy training had something to do with that. But when she saw me standing on her porch, she burst into tears. So, yeah, I think Edmund was heading home. He'd had enough. He'd found out enough about himself he didn't need to look any further.

The time was later than I realized. I'd gotten lost in my reverie. Cal would be here any moment.

"Here you are," Tina said. "I thought you were leaving."

"I was. I am. I asked Mrs. Lowell for a list of the dates and places Edmund called from. I was looking it over and got lost in thought."

She came over to my desk and took a look. "Mostly called from California," she said. "Makes sense." She looked closer. "Huh. Looks like he was heading home."

"My thoughts exactly."

The doorbell rang.

"That's probably Cal," I said. "I'd best get going."

"You sure you won't stay?"

"Look, you and Cal don't want me hanging around."

"Harry…"

The doorbell rang again.

We walked to the foyer.

Tina opened the door. Cal was on the front step, two big pizza boxes in his hands.

"About time you answered the door," he said. "Thought I was going to have to eat this myself."

Tina invited him in. When he saw me, he said, "I wasn't sure if you were going to be here or not, that's why I got two. Jakeeno's. I know how you love the place."

And I do.

"Harry isn't staying," Tina said.

"What?" Cal replied. "C'mon, Major. Got this just for you."

"Are you sure?" I asked.

"Look, Harry, do I have to handcuff you to something?"

"I just don't want to be a fifth wheel."

"For God's sake, man, I need you around to help keep the Red Baron in line."

I laughed. "All right, then. Jakeeno's pizza and a plea for help. How can I refuse?"

Yes, sirree. I hope Tina and Cal get married. We're already like a family.

4

GWEN AND TATTY

SATURDAY, OCTOBER 6TH

I WAS UP EARLY and a good thing, too. Ed Hafner was ringing our doorbell at seven in the morning.

"I'm really sorry, Harry, but I got a job I hafta start at eight and I wanted to get this to you ASAP."

I nodded, said, "C'mon in," and he followed me to the office, where he proceeded to tell me about his night.

"I went to them two shelters like you wanted. One fella, a regular, recognized the beard picture. He said he'd seen Eddie, he called him that, sometime end of June, beginning of July. Remembers he went off with Brother Leonard. Didn't see him after that."

"Thanks, Ed."

"Uh, I also spread around thirty-eight Jacksons."

"No problem. How many hours?"

"Six and a half."

I paid him three hundred and ninety dollars for his time and reimbursed him for the Andy Jacksons he'd spread around for good will. He thanked me and took off. I recorded the expense, put the book away, and my cell chimed. Stinky sent a text asking when would be a good time to stop by. I texted back and told him anytime was fine. He replied he'd be at our place around ten.

The kids would be up in another hour or two, which meant I'd best get breakfast going. The pizza leftovers I put in the fridge. The empty beer and wine bottles into the recycling. The dirty dishes into the dishwasher. I made tea and considered what to make for breakfast. Kielbasa and buckwheat pancakes sounded good to me, so I got started.

Cal was first down. "Hey, Major."

"Morning, Cal."

"You were sound asleep in your rocking chair. Hope you don't mind our not disturbing you."

"No. No problem."

"I wanted to wake you, but Tina said no." He poured himself tea.

"You have to go in today?" I asked.

"Not unless someone ends up dead."

"Looking to be a cold, dreary day."

"That it is. You working?"

"We have the skip trace. Stinky Johnson will be by a little later."

"Yeah. Tina was telling me you haven't gotten too far. These skip traces can be real pissers."

"Certainly can be." I finished cooking the pancakes and sausage. "Come on, let's eat."

We sat down, and Tina showed up.

Cal laughed. "Why is it the Red Baron always shows up when the food is ready?"

I smiled, and Tina gave him the finger.

"Guess she's not too talkative this morning," Cal said, and conveyed a big wedge of pancake to his mouth.

"Never is," I said. "But you should realize that by now."

"Yeah, I should," he said around a bite of kielbasa. "Slow learner when it comes to women."

I offered Cal the newspaper, and he took the sports section. I skimmed through news articles and op eds. Tina poured herself tea, took one pancake and one sausage, and buried her nose in her iPad. Cal and I swapped news items. He sports, I world events until we had eaten our fill and called this breakfast history. Tina stood and announced she would be in the office. I told her Stinky was stopping by around ten. She nodded and left.

I started picking up the dishes, and Cal helped.

"She really isn't a morning person, is she?" he said.

"Nope. Never was. Even when a kid."

"So it's not me."

"No. Not you."

"She's like that with…"

"Yep. Doesn't matter who's here. Even God gets the same treatment."

He chuckled. "Good to know I'm on par with the Almighty."

I smiled. "Isn't it though? And for what it's worth, she really, I mean really, likes you. And if you ask me, she loves you."

"Thanks, Harry, for that tidbit. It's also comforting to find out that after all these years it isn't me. She just doesn't like mornings."

The dining room cleaned up, he asked if I wanted him to help with dishes or anything. I told him I had it under control. He said he was joining Tina in the office. I got the kitchen cleaned up and joined them.

"Ed was here at seven with his report," I said.

Tina lit a cigar and poured herself a glass of madeira.

Cal waved his hand. "Geez, Wright, isn't it a little early?"

"If you don't like it, Swenson, you know where the door is."

He looked at me.

I said, "Ignore these comments."

He smiled and said, "Okay, Wright, I guess we get lung cancer together."

"I don't inhale," she said.

"Okay, I get the lung cancer and you get mouth, lip, and throat cancer. Can we die in each other's arms?"

"Sure," she replied, and smiled. "I'd like that."

I interrupted their jocularity with work. "Ed said he found someone who remembered seeing Edmund for the last time around the end of June or the beginning of July. He, that is Edmund, went off with Brother Leonard and wasn't seen after that."

"Interesting. We need info on this 'Brother Leonard' character."

The doorbell rang. Ten o'clock. Probably Stinky and right on the dot.

When I opened the door, he said, "Good morning, Harry."

"A good morning to you, Stinky." I let him in. He was attired in an impeccable navy suit, white shirt, repp tie, and black oxfords. He followed me into the office, his black trilby in his hand.

"Good morning Miss Wright, Lieutenant Swenson."

"Hi Stinky," Cal replied.

Tina echoed his good morning.

"I found two men who recognized the missing person. One recognized the clean shaven picture, but couldn't remember when he saw the subject. The other recognized the bearded photo and said he saw the subject on July fourth when he was leaving with Brother Leonard."

Tina nodded. "So it seems July fourth is the last we can

establish that anyone saw Edmund alive in Minneapolis." She puffed on her cigar and said, "We need to find out who this Brother Leonard is."

"I asked about him," Stinky said. "He's apparently a worker over in Economic Assistance. Always trying to help the homeless."

"Do you have a last name on him?" Tina asked.

"That's a bit sketchy," Stinky replied, "Johnson and Thompson were the most common replies the men came up with. Although one thought Arneson and another Levinson."

Cal asked, "Didn't any of them have him for a worker?"

Stinky explained, "The workers don't have their own case-loads anymore. They work in teams. So a client ends up seeing anyone on the team."

"I see," Cal said.

Tina was all smiles. Which was something considering the time was still morning. "We can start working on this. Thanks, Stinky."

"You're welcome, Miss Wright. I also passed out eleven ten-dollar bills."

"We'll reimburse you," I said. "How many hours did you work?"

"Seven and three quarters."

I paid him in cash for eight at Ed's rate, which is at least twenty an hour more than what Stinky usually gets, and reimbursed him for the tens he gave away.

"Thank you very much, Harry." He stuck out his hand, and I took it.

"My pleasure, Stinky. You got us good info. Thanks."

"My pleasure as well," he replied. "A good day to you, Miss Wright, Lieutenant Swenson."

I walked him out to the door and returned to the office.

"So now what?" I asked.

"We did what the police didn't do, and that has given us two pieces of information," Tina said. "Number one, Edmund was last seen by the homeless community on Independence Day. And number two, he went off with Brother Leonard. I think it is reasonable to assume Brother Leonard is somehow connected with Edmund's disappearance. Whether or not there has been foul play remains to be seen."

"Sounds good to me," Cal said.

"Are we still pursuing Lowell and Osgood?" I asked.

"We know Osgood felt threatened by Edmund. We also know something occurred between Lowell and his son which resulted in the son leaving."

"Uh, we don't know that," I said. "We've inferred something happened between Lowell and Edmund that was beyond their normal dysfunctional relationship."

"All right," Tina said, "I suspect something happened between Lowell and his son which may or may not provide us with a solution to the case."

"Aren't this Osgood and Lowell in Ohio?" Cal asked.

Tina confirmed they were.

Cal continued, "Then I think you could send someone to Ohio to check them out while you work on the Brother Leonard angle here."

Tina nodded. "I like it, Sweet Cheeks, although Minnesota has no reciprocity agreement with Ohio. Or any other state, for that matter." She thought a minute. Looked at me. Looked at the ceiling. Finally her eyes met mine and she said, "I'd like to send David Nagasawa because Lowell knows what we look like. But I want you to see if Gwen Poisson is available. I have a feeling a woman might get better results and I think she might be licensed in Ohio."

I picked up my cell and said, "Call Gwen Poisson." David

Nagasawa just might be the best operative this side of either coast. David asks for and gets a hundred and twenty-five an hour. Gwen Poisson is a computer whiz and generally works for Leigh Bjork's or Fred Langley's agencies. If she's available, she'll always work on an assignment for Tina. She usually gets eighty an hour and is second only to David. She answered on the fifth ring.

"Hi, Gwen. Harry Wright."

"Hey, Harry. How's it going?"

"Good. Say, Tina has a job for you if you are available."

"Finished one up for Fred yesterday. I'm available."

"Good. Why don't you come over and let Tina explain what she wants?"

"Sure. Give me an hour, maybe hour and a half."

"See you then."

We ended the call and I let Tina know Gwen would be gracing us with her presence in an hour to hour and a half.

"Good. We'll let Gwen tackle my suspicions in Ohio and you and I, Harry, will tackle the mysterious Brother Leonard here."

Cal chimed in, "The first thing you're going to need is a good name for this guy."

I quickly brought up the Hennepin County website. "I don't see a county employee directory online. Just a number to call. And I doubt they're going to want to do a lot of searching for us."

"I'll check with a friend of mine in the Sheriff's office and see if he has access to the county's internal phone directory," Cal said.

"Thanks, Sweet Cheeks," Tina replied.

"Don't want to derail the General when she's on a roll," he added. He looked at his watch. "When's Gwen going to be here?"

I looked at my desk clock. "Should be here within the next forty-five minutes."

"I think I'm going to head out. Have some things to do around the house. I'll call you later, Buttercup."

"Don't forget," Tina said.

He moved around Tina's desk, gave her a kiss, and headed for the door. "See ya, Harry."

"Catch you later, Cal." I followed him out to make sure the door was closed and returned to the office.

Standing in the doorway, I said, "Lunchtime is nearly upon us. Do you want to wait until after Gwen leaves?"

"Yes. Let's wait."

I sat at my desk and thought about Brother Leonard. Tina picked up her book. And thus we occupied ourselves until the doorbell rang, and I ushered Gwen Poisson into the office.

Gwen is forty. She stands five-four, with an average frame, and wears her dark chocolate hair in a pixie cut. She worked ten years out in Silicon Valley, another three as a professional hacker, before becoming a PI.

"What do you have for me?" she asked. Her voice is light enough to be unmistakably feminine and has enough depth to give it a touch of sultry mystery.

Tina explained our case and what we'd found out thus far. "However, I can't shake the feeling Lowell and Osgood may somehow be involved in the picture somewhere."

"And you want me to find out if there is a connection someplace," Gwen added.

"Yes."

"You have pictures of these guys?"

"Unfortunately, no."

"That's okay. I'll work around it."

"I'd like you to start as soon as possible. You're licensed in Ohio, aren't you?"

"Yes. I'm close to a cousin in Cleveland and got licensed there. I stay with her on occasion and get in some work in The Buckeye State. I'll look into a flight to Cincy tomorrow or Monday. Anything else?"

"No. Just work your magic."

Gwen smiled. "That I always do."

I fixed her up with cash and a credit card. She thanked us for the work and said she'd keep us posted. I walked her to the door, she gave me a hug, and left. Nice woman. A little too green and vegan for my taste, but a lovely person.

When I returned to the office, Tina said, "Let's get lunch. I'll drive."

"Not in the mood for leftovers?"

"No. I'd just like to go out."

"Okay."

Tina took out the Thunderbird and drove us over to Clancey's for sandwiches. I also bought sausage as long as we were there.

"We need to ID this Brother Leonard and then we need to talk to him," she said.

"Agreed."

"I think, if he's available, we should have Stinky ID the guy; and if Ed is available, he can do surveillance on our Brother Leonard."

"I agree."

"Well, then, you know what you have to do after lunch."

And I told her we were in agreement on that as well.

We ate our sandwiches and returned to Tina's pile on West Franklin. She decided to spend the remainder of the afternoon painting and I made phone calls. Ed was working and said he'd get back to me later. Stinky said he'd probably be able to work for us next week. He'd let us know on Monday. And there we were. I was very tempted to see what I could locate on my own. Although I have to admit, Stinky has a rapport with that group of people that I don't have. So maybe I should just sit tight and wait. And after thinking about it, I decided that's exactly what I'd do. I checked the theaters, found one still showing *Solomon Kane*, and told Tina I'd be gone for the evening.

"By yourself?" she asked.

"Yes. I have no partner and I'd rather not pay for a Rent A Friend and you wouldn't be interested in the movie."

"There's such a thing as Rent A Friend?"

"There is. It's a place to find a buddy with whom to do something. And not sex. It's purely platonic."

"Learn something new every day. Well, have fun."

"I will. Catch you later."

I grabbed my car keys and a coat. I had plenty of time before the show and thought to spend the time perusing the offerings of one of my favorite used bookstores. Uncle Hugo's and Uncle Edgar's are Minneapolis landmarks. If you love books, particularly sci-fi, fantasy, and mysteries, you'll love Uncle H and Uncle E. Sometimes a person will enter the door and not be seen again for days. So that didn't happen to me, I set the alarm on my phone.

Up and down the rows I walked, looked through piles of books stacked on the floor, picked out several to take home with me, and moved on to the mystery section. I found Ngaio Marsh and was trying to remember if the book I was looking at was already in my collection, when someone tapped my shoulder.

I turned around.

"I thought that was you." Her English was flavored with a Hungarian accent.

"Tatty! What a surprise."

Tatiana Bogar, a Hungarian here on a student visa, is a

woman FIDE Master and plays a mean game of chess. I've never beaten her, but have gotten a couple of draws. And lost at least a dozen games. She's nineteen, and quite attractive.

She gave me a hug. "You are looking for books?" Then embarrassed by the obviousness of the answer, said, "Of course. This is a bookstore."

"I'm trying to remember if I have this book or not. Have you found anything?"

"Yes." She showed me.

"Ah, Cordwainer Smith. Good stuff."

"I never heard of him."

That was all I needed, and I launched into a discussion of Smith's importance to the world of science fiction. I didn't get too far when the alarm on my phone sounded.

"Ah, my time's up. Have to get a bite to eat before the movie."

"What movie are you going to?"

"*Solomon Kane.*"

"I did not see it. Are you with someone?"

"No. Just myself."

"You go to movies by yourself?"

"Sometimes." Why I asked, I don't know. I'm three and a half decades older than she is. But ask I did. "Would you like to join me?"

She smiled. "Yes. Do you mind?"

"Not at all. If you don't mind being seen with an old guy."

"You're not an old man. Middle age. Besides, we're friends."

"Let's get something to eat before the show starts."

We paid for our books and I took her to a decent restaurant. The movie was not bad. Fairly violent. Touching love story. Tatty drives but doesn't have a car or Minnesota license and had taken the bus to the bookstore. So when the movie was over, I was going to take her to her house.

She said, "My roommates will be there. Maybe we can play chess at your place?"

I considered her request for a moment, before saying, "Sure. My sister and her friend might be home. But she has a very big house." So I drove on home.

When we arrived, Tatty said, "This is a very big house. Your sister must be rich."

"Not really. She won't say where she got the money to buy it. But she makes enough to pay the taxes."

I made tea for us, and when it was ready we moved from the kitchen to the game room. Tina wasn't home, so I assumed she was out with Cal. Tatty gave me pawn and move odds in our first game. I played aggressively to take advantage of the hole on her f7 square, but she parried effectively. In the end we agreed to call the game a draw.

I got out my chess clock. "I'm horrible at blitz. How about I get forty-five minutes—"

"And I'll get ten."

"Ten?"

She nodded.

"Okay." I set the times on the clocks, and she set up the board.

We drew for colors and I got black. She pushed her pawn to e4, I pushed mine to e5, and she played her knight to f3. I took a deep breath and played my pawn to f5, the infamous Latvian Gambit.

She smiled and said, "Here we go again. You are... How do you say? Glutton for punishment?"

I laughed. "I guess so."

She paused a moment and then played her knight to e3 and I countered with my pawn to d6. Tatty took thirty seconds before playing her pawn to d4. We were now playing the Philidor Counter-Attack.

I pushed the game hard and was threatening to break through on the kingside.

She was down to two minutes and I still had twenty. She stared at the board. Two minutes became one minute. One minute became thirty seconds. She moved.

I pressed my attack. She sacrificed a bishop. Now my turn. Four minutes passed. I didn't see what she was up to. I played, continuing my attack. She sacked a rook. Uh-oh. I was in trouble.

Ten minutes passed on my clock. I was in hot water. Finally I pushed a rook.

She moved. I moved. She moved and had ten seconds remaining. I was down to two minutes. I moved.

Tatty smiled, let the clock get down to two seconds, moved, and said, "Mate."

I shook my head. I was the one who'd gotten flustered by the time crunch.

She leaned across the board and kissed me. Soft and gentle. I was surprised. We were friends, but not that kind of friends. She looked at me, searching my face.

"Uh, Tatty—"

I didn't get to finish. She kissed me again. Her lips slightly parted and I knew then the double entendre behind her use of the word "mate."

5

SPELUNKING AND CHESS
MONDAY - TUESDAY, OCTOBER 8TH - 9TH

I MUST'VE FELT her looking at me, for when I looked up from the computer sure enough she was indeed looking at me.

"What?" I said.

She shook her head, blew smoke towards the ceiling, and said, "I'm still a bit in shock over yesterday morning."

"I slept with a woman. It's happened before, you know."

Tina nodded. "I'd assumed so. You were married. But to find at our breakfast table someone who could possibly be my daughter, well…" She shrugged. "Cal was speechless."

"Yeah. I know. I was there. Look. Tatty and I are chess buddies. She was missing her boyfriend back in Hungary and was tired of the battery operated one over here. Probably won't happen again."

The phone rang. Ah, saved. I answered, "Wright Investigations."

"Harry, this is Stinky. I'm available tonight."

"Great. Tina wants you to get the lowdown on this Brother Leonard. Full name, where he works, address, you name it."

"I'll see what I can do. I'll let you know tomorrow morning what I came up with."

"Thanks, Stinky."

I ended the call, and my cell chimed. I looked down at who the text was from. Gwen. The message was simple:

> In Cincy. Airline FUBB. Lost bag. Waiting to
> see if they find it. VSF. TTYL. Gwen.

"Stinky is available tonight and will see what he can find. Gwen's in Cincinnati hoping the airline finds her bag."

Tina nodded.

My phone rang again. Cal. I answered, and he said, "Hey Major. No luck from my buddy in the sheriff's office getting a phone number on your guy. Sorry about that."

"Not a prob. We'll get it."

"I'm sure you will," he replied, and rang off.

I relayed the info to Tina, and she nodded to acknowledge she heard me.

"Well, I guess there's not much—" My cell chimed informing me I had an email. I checked and saw a message from Tatty. How odd. She gave no indication Saturday night was anything more than an adventure in lust. So why would she be emailing? I read the letter.

"Tatty just sent me an invitation to join her and her friends tonight to go exploring manmade caves."

"The batteries probably died."

"Good grief." Tatty had included her phone number so I could call her back with my decision. I punched the numbers. She answered on the second ring.

"Hello?"

"Hi, Tatty. Harry here."

"Hi, Harry! Do you want to go exploring with us?"

"What are you exploring?"

"Urban caves. Tonight the ones under the U's St. Paul campus."

"Is that legal?"

"No. If you don't want to go with us, that is okay."

I thought a bit. Long enough for Tatty to check if I was still there.

"I'm here. Sure. I'll go."

"Will you pick me up?"

"Sure. What time?"

"Ten tonight."

"See you then."

"Bye." And she ended the call.

"You, my stodgy brother, are going to do something illegal?"

"I guess I am."

"And you're going with the girl who could be my daughter?"

"Oh, stop it already."

Clearly Tina was enjoying this, chortling away while trying to read her book. I got up and left. Enough is enough. I am not a daredevil. But to be honest, I'd always wanted to try spelunking. I figured how difficult would it be to explore underground manmade tunnels? Better than diving into a pond to gain entrance to a cave, right? Of course. Especially given I can't swim. Anyway, I was hoping for a little adventure I could brag about in my old age with suitable embellishments and monsters worthy of Lovecraft, Howard, or King. And what's the harm in that?

———

I picked Tatty up at ten. She was ready and dressed for a night of grunging.

"I brought a helmet for you," she said.

"Thanks. Hadn't thought of that. How long have you been a caver?"

"Three years. I enjoy almost as much as chess."

"But why not a real cave?"

"Oh, I explore those as well. There are many natural and manmade caves right here underneath the Twin Cities."

"I didn't know that."

"Hardly anyone does. They are illegal to explore and often very dangerous. But people do explore them."

"And these are real caves?"

"Some are. Much of the time they have sewage water in them because they've been made part of the city's sewers."

"You didn't—"

She laughed. "No sewage where we are going."

That was a relief to hear.

"Are you a geology major by chance?" I asked.

"Yes."

"Figures."

"The earth is where we live. Geology helps us to understand."

"I suppose it does. Are there lots of these underground places beneath the Twin Cities?"

"Oh, yes. Especially St. Paul."

"I would have never guessed."

We parked on the neighborhood streets off Raymond where we met Logan, another caver, and Cynice, who is a student at the Ag school. We started walking the several blocks to the heating plant.

Logan informed us, "There was a group in the Cities ten to twenty years ago that used to go exploring. They're no longer active, but their website is. That's where I got the idea to explore some of the sights. Unfortunately, time moves on and some of the places have been demolished or access has been blocked off."

"But the steam tunnels are still here," Cynice said.

"That they are." There was a big smile on Logan's face.

––––––

Someday I may write up my adventure in the steam tunnels under the U of M St. Paul campus. Suffice it to say the adventure was interesting and exciting, especially the part when we were chased by the campus police. The four of us fled in different directions, which allowed us to evade the watchdogs. When I got back to my car, Tatty was waiting. Logan and Cynice had just taken off.

"They offered me a ride, but I said I'd wait for you."

"You could've gone with them and texted me."

"I know."

We got into my Focus, and I turned the car back towards Minneapolis. We didn't say much about the night's adventure. The air between us seemed charged. I felt something of relief and sadness when I turned down her street.

"Harry, will you take me home with you?"

I stopped the car in the middle of the street and looked at her. She looked at me and then out the windshield. I touched her cheek, and my fingers became wet with her tears. She took my hand.

"I'm homesick, Harry. Please."

"You sure, Tatty?"

She nodded.

I made a u-turn and drove to Tina's place. The house was dark. Being two in the morning, I wasn't surprised. I unlocked the door, reset the alarm, and let Tatty in. We climbed the stairs to my room, stripped out of our dirty clothes, showered together, made love, and slept together.

In the morning, later in the morning actually, I laid out a robe for her to wear when she woke up and took our clothes downstairs to the basement to wash. While the washer was doing its thing, I made tea and breakfast. She came down an hour later. The clothes were in the dryer by then.

"You must think poorly of me," she said.

"No more poorly than I think of myself."

"I love Lazlo, Harry. I want you to know that."

"I understand. We're still chess buddies, aren't we?"

She smiled. "Yes, chess buddies."

"Your clothes should be almost dry by now."

"Thank you."

"Don't mention it. It's what buddies do."

"Yes. It's what buddies do."

"Tea?"

She nodded. I poured her a cup, and she sat on a barstool while I checked the dryer. The clothes were dry, and I brought them up.

"Here you go, Tatty."

"Thank you." She put her arms around me and hugged me. "I have class. I should go."

"I'll give you a ride to the campus."

"Thanks."

She took her clothes and went upstairs to dress. Tina came down and sat in the dining room. I brought her toast and tea. She gave me a puzzled look.

"I have to run Tatty to school. I'll be back."

She raised her eyebrows but said nothing.

I ran Tatiana to the U and when I got back Tina was in the office. I took tea and a turnover to my desk.

"Is this a new routine?"

"No. Tatty made it clear she loves her boyfriend back home, which I take to mean whatever itch she had has been scratched."

Tina nodded. "Have fun last night?"

"Too much fun. Almost got caught by campus police."

"That wouldn't have been good for business."

"No. It wouldn't." My phone beeped. A text from Gwen. "Gwen says she finally got her bag and is on her way to Dayton."

"Good."

The phone beeped again. "Stinky will be by around ten-thirty to give us his report."

"Very good."

I looked at the computer screen, but wasn't seeing anything. Tatty may have scratched her itch, but now I had the itch. I wiped away a tear running down my cheek.

"She's awfully young for you, Harry."

"I know."

"Maybe it's time you started dating."

"No."

"Suit yourself. Having someone can be quite pleasant."

"Yeah. I know."

Tina knows when not to talk and she let the subject drop. I was feeling like a fool. An old fool. The worst kind. I got up and slowly walked to the kitchen. I poured tea. Took a deep breath and another turnover and returned to the office to wait for Stinky.

The doorbell rang promptly at ten-thirty. I ushered Stinky into the office. We exchanged good mornings and then he began his report.

"I found a man and two staffers who confirmed Brother Leonard's last name to be Johnson. One of the staffers, Pedro

Garcia, with the aid of Ben and his twin, said he's helped Brother Leonard to find suitable homeless men on occasion."

Tina asked if Stinky knew what he meant by "suitable".

"Yes, I asked him. He said they had to be healthy and able to work. He, that is Brother Leonard, especially wanted to help those who had no family." Stinky passed a couple of printed sheets to Tina. "It's all there. No one knew his home address, but I got his work phone and his work address."

"Thanks, Stinky. This is very helpful."

"You're welcome, Miss Wright."

I paid Stinky in cash and he was off.

"Now what?" I asked.

"We need a picture of Brother Leonard and we set a tail on him."

"How do you propose to get a picture of him?"

"Interview him."

"You or me?"

"I'll interview him. I'm a woman. He's a man. Instant draw."

"Good luck."

"Harry, why don't you take the day off?"

"I'm okay, Tina. This isn't the first time I've been disappointed. My own fault. I knew she was using me. I'm the one who let my feelings get a bit out of control. I'll be fine."

"Okay." She looked at the papers Stinky had given her, punched numbers into a cell, and waited. Then she said, her voice cane syrup and magnolias, "Hello, Mr. Johnson. My name is Georgia Brown. I'm a doctoral student at the U and I'd like to interview you about your work with the homeless. My number is—" She told him her phone number and hung up.

"Why the Southern Belle?"

"Men love it. They think you're dumb, naïve, and easily manipulated into bed."

"I see."

"Even if they don't take advantage, it helps to manipulate a man if you let him think there is a possibility he might, under the right circumstances, get a piece of ass."

"Hope it works."

In her best cane syrup and magnolia twang, she said, "Oh, it does, Honey. It does."

6

LUNCH WITH LEONARD JOHNSON

WEDNESDAY, OCTOBER 10TH

THE SUN TRIED ITS BEST, but in the end the clouds won. No golden rays to light up the afternoon. Tina, however, was quite sunny. Her southern belle charm had worked its magic, plus a few tips from Dale Carnegie. She puffed away on a cigar and sipped on a glass of madeira.

"Where did you go for lunch?" I asked.

"The Local. He even bought."

"Wow. I'm impressed. Did he ask you any questions?"

"He did. He asked if I was married, and why I was working on a doctorate. I told him I wasn't, and I wanted a leg up going into social work. Everyone has her masters today."

I nodded.

"Then I got him talking about himself, his job, his work with the homeless, my chances of getting work at the county, and I got a picture."

"And?"

"I can call him anytime."

"I meant his work."

"Oh, that? Nothing special. He's a Human Services Representative. He determines eligibility for welfare programs. But what I found interesting is he was quite vague about his work with the homeless. I did my best to pin him down, but each time he slipped away. All he would say is he had some connections with employers out west. Developed when he lived out there. Wouldn't tell me who they were. He takes the best prospects, and pays for a one-way bus ticket, and leaves the rest to the employers. He provides a bed and food while here and assesses their job skills. Then contacts the potential employers."

"So what do you think?"

"He's lying through his teeth. There's something phony about the story."

"If it's a lie, what does he do with the homeless guys?"

"That's a good question, Harry. A very good question." She puffed on her cigar and sipped madeira. "He knows me. So, I'm out. I want you to tail him. If they're available, I also want David, Ed, and Stinky."

"No holds barred."

"I need to get intel on this guy. I don't know how he's involved with our subject, but apparently he is. Before I ask him, I want to know him inside and out."

"When do you want me to start the tail?"

"ASAP. He's at the Century Plaza building now, unless he's already left for the day. On second thought, tomorrow morning. See if you can get the boys and check out what you can find on little Len from the computer."

"Gotcha."

Unfortunately, the best laid plans of mice and men usually fall victim to Murphy. David wasn't free until Saturday. Ed was on a job and thought he might be free Friday. If not, then Monday. The weekend was out. Stinky had a surveillance job and wouldn't be available until next week at the earliest. That left moi. I'd be doing surveillance by myself of a building covering an entire city block. How do you spell impossible? I informed Tina, and she nodded.

I turned to the computer and attempted to locate info on our Leonard Johnson. I found fifty-three of them. When I ruled out those who lived out of state or were too old, I'd narrowed the field down to eight. Thank God Leonard is mostly an old man's name. What I needed was his home address. That would have to wait until I, or one of the guys followed him home.

"No sense sitting here," I told Tina. "I'll scope out the building."

She nodded, and I grabbed my hat and coat and left. I parked by the convention center and began walking around the welfare building. At ten after four, people were going in and out in significant numbers. This would not be easy. I saw lots of Somalis and heard lots of Spanish. White males seemed almost as common as parrots in Antarctica. That was a plus since Len was a white male.

One set of doors on Third and two sets on each of the other two sides. Small parking lot on Fourth with a loading bay and two more entrances. The entrance to the parking ramp inside the building was on Twelfth. Too many ways in and out of the building. We'd need at least four people. More if we wanted a break.

I started thinking who else could I call while I took a stroll around the place. I tried the doors on the Eleventh Street side and found them locked. No entrance from that direction. The doors on Fourth were similarly locked, although one had badge access for workers. But the loading dock door was open, so anyone could go in or out. The Twelfth Street doors weren't locked either, however the parking ramp entrance would allow anyone to enter or exit the place.

My conclusion? In the morning there'd most likely be

restricted entrance, at least until business hours. But anyone could leave by any door anytime of the day. We might be able to get by with a small surveillance team in the morning. Might.

Part of the problem facing us was we didn't know where to look for him. Did he drive to work, bus to work, walk, bicycle? We didn't know. If he arrived before business hours, he had the front door, the rear card access door, and likely the parking ramp entrance. Tomorrow morning I'd camp out at the front door. As good a place as any to start.

I walked back to my car and drove home. At least Tina got a picture of him. Now I had to study it and fix it in my mind. If I caught him going into the place, then I just had to catch him coming out when he was heading home and follow him to his car or the bus. If his car, I knew where he parked; the make, year, and model; and most important, the license plate number. If the bus, I followed him home or to his car. Not difficult. Just tedious.

But detective work is by and large tedious routine. And most of the clients, monotonously boring. I can't say I enjoy detective work. Then again, I don't like putting puzzles together either. Yet, I love chess. Go figure.

Tina was in the living room reading by the fire and eating a bowl of NuNus and hot dogs for supper. "Rather a challenge, isn't it?" she said.

"It is."

"I used street view to look at the place while you were out." She got a fork loaded up with noodles. "I figure six to observe all the doors."

"Yeah. Probably. Certainly around quitting time."

"I also made a phone call. They work weird hours over there. Some kind of flexible scheduling."

"Great. That's all we need."

"Don't worry, Harry. I'll help you out. I'll just have to dress down. You and I will keep the place under surveillance until we can get additional troops."

"Going to get your hands dirty. You haven't done that for a while."

"Did it too much in the CIA. However, this should be tame enough."

We agreed we'd monitor the Third Avenue entrance and the Fourth Avenue entrance in the morning. In the afternoon, we'd focus on the Twelfth Street entrance closest to Third and the Third Avenue entrance with an eye towards the Eleventh Street door closest to Third. We figured it was the best we could do.

Then I got an idea. "Remember Sherlock Holmes?"

"Well, yes. What about him?"

"The Baker Street Irregulars."

"Okay. Where are you going with this?"

"College students need money. Let's say twenty an hour and we can perhaps cover all the doors."

"Tatty. You sly devil."

"Not that. We can use her eyes and those of her friends."

"They're not trained. Yet, it might work. Call her."

I called Tatiana. The first moment or two were awkward, but we got over it and I told her what we needed and if she and her friends could help. "Five hours or so at twenty an hour," I said. "A hundred bucks. What do you say?"

"Tomorrow?"

"Yes. And possibly the day after."

"I will help. I'll ask around to see if anyone else wants to help."

"Thanks, Tatty."

"Uh, Harry, I'm very sorry."

"Tatty. You've nothing to be sorry for. We're fine."

"Thank you. Because I very much like you."

"I very much like you, as well. We're good."

"Thank you. I'll let you know."

We ended the call, and I told Tina she'd call me back and let me know if we had any takers. She nodded.

My phone beeped. A text message from Gwen. She was in Dayton and ready to begin. I passed the info on to Tina.

"Thanks, Harry. I'm going to play some music before hitting the hay. We should probably go to bed early since we have to be up early tomorrow. Don't want to miss him because we were yawning."

"Right. I'm going to have a glass of port, after which I'll follow suit."

She nodded and went to the music room. From the sound of the music, it was something by Mozart.

I poured myself a glass of port and sat in the rocking chair in the living room. I sipped wine, gazed at the fire, and thought about the case. I didn't finish the wine, though. Fell asleep and might have remained in my chair if my phone hadn't rung at midnight and woken me up.

"Harry, Tat here. Sorry to call so late. I got Logan and Cynice and another friend, Crystal. Where and when should we meet you?"

"Meet Tina and me by the Lutheran church on Twelfth and Third at noon."

"Okay. See you then."

"Bye."

I suppose I'll have to call them the Franklin Street Irregulars. Or maybe the West Franklin Irregulars. In either case, we got our group. And I was going to bed for five hours.

7

SOMETIMES FORTUNA SMILES

FRIDAY, OCTOBER 12TH

Sometimes Fortuna smiles, and Murphy has to get into the backseat. Maybe even the trunk. That happened today in the late afternoon. Tina got to do her happy dance.

Thursday, noon, the "Irregulars" showed up at the Lutheran church. Tatty and I made introductions. I handed out copies of the photo of our subject.

Logan said, "This guy was out caving with us a couple times." He couldn't remember his name. When I told him, he replied, "Yeah, now I remember. He said his name was Lonnie."

"How long ago was it he went caving?" Tina asked.

"Three summers ago, I think," Logan said.

I explained what we wanted done and asked if there were questions.

Cynice said, "So, if we see this guy we just follow him?"

"Correct," Tina answered. "But whatever you do, don't get made. He can't know you're following him."

Crystal asked, "And if he gets on a bus? Like what then?"

"Follow him," Tina said. "I need his home address."

"If he gets into a car, get the license plate number," I added.

"That's most important," Tina said. "Then the make, model, and year."

Tina took the Third Avenue door, and I took the door on Twelfth by the ramp entrance. Logan had the Eleventh Street doors, Tatty and Cynice the Fourth Avenue doors, and Crystal the other door on Twelfth.

We were at our posts by twelve-thirty. We watched and waited. And watched and waited some more. I made periodic phone calls to make sure the "Irregulars" stayed awake. And vigilant. Then we watched and waited some more.

But by Thursday's end, we had nothing. I asked if they were available Friday and all were, so I gave each of them forty dollars and said they'd get the rest on Friday at the end of the day. Crystal put up a bit of a fuss, but Tatty assured her we were good for the money.

Before getting into Logan's car, Tatty touched my sleeve and said, "Nice to see you, Harry. Really. Thanks. On the Get Rooked site, I'm Tat Trap. Let's play a game." I assured her I would, and she got into Logan's car. They left and Tina and I got into her Thunderbird.

On the way home we swung by White Castle, got sliders and fries, and ate them in the car.

"What did Tatiana say?" Tina asked.

"That it was nice to see me and invited me to play chess with her on a website."

"She doesn't want to let you go. At least not totally."

"Keep her boyfriend at home and her fuck buddy in Minneapolis."

"I think she views you as safe. You aren't going to want to marry her and she isn't going to want to marry you. Yeah. You're a buddy. Not a lover. A friend with benefits. I guess you have to decide if you want the benefits."

I ate french fries. Mostly because they were good, but also so I didn't have to answer.

Did I want a friend with benefits? Sometimes the benefits leave you feeling more empty than you were before you enjoyed them. Kind of making them counterproductive.

I was conflicted. I liked Tatty. I liked her a lot. But she'd always just been the girl at the chess club or online who was a damn good player. Then suddenly we have sex and my world, and I think hers, too, is upside down. I sighed. Probably best if I ignore her and move on.

Today, which also happens to be my birthday, saw Tina and I once again having the old Century Plaza building under surveillance, starting very early in the morning. At six-ten I spotted a man I thought might be our subject, but he was too far away to be sure in the dusky light. He turned on Third and entered the Third Avenue door. Tina wasn't able to get a good look at him to confirm if he was our subject or not.

A little before ten the wind picked up. The temp slowly climbed through the forties, but the wind made surveillance nasty.

At noon, the "Irregulars" arrived. Tina shuffled everyone around. She put Crystal on Fourth. Tatty on Eleventh. Cynice on the corner of Eleventh and Fourth. Logan by the ramp entrance. I had Third, and she had the other Twelfth Street entrance. And we waited and waited and waited some more.

At five-thirty, Tatty texted that she saw Lonnie leave the building by the Eleventh Street door near Third and she was following. I was closest and texted back I'd join in the tailing. I jogged over to Eleventh, spotted Tatty, and our subject. I was behind him, and she was pacing him on the other side of the street. At Nicollet Mall, he waited for the light before crossing the street. I remained behind him and Tatty turned the corner and walked down the mall a ways.

When the light changed, he crossed the street and turned into The Local. I phoned Tina and told her where we were at, then I motioned for Tatty to join me and we followed him inside. Lonnie was at the bar and had a beer in front of him. We took a table and pretty soon a coffee was on the table before Tatty and a tea on the table before me. We said nothing. Just watched our subject.

Close to half an hour passed before he finished his beer and stood. I put a ten on the table, and when he was out the door, we followed. He turned the corner, and we hurried after him.

Our disadvantage lay in our now being on the same side of the street. We followed him down to Marquette and mingled with the good citizens of Minneapolis clustered around the same bus stop Lonnie had chosen. I called Tina to let her know where we were.

When I put the cell back in my pocket, Tatty whispered, "What language was that you were speaking?"

"Esperanto. Taught it to Tina when she was a kid. It was the hope of the future. One happy world, all speaking the same language. Today, hardly anyone has heard of it. Gone the way of the dinosaur. Comes in handy, though."

"I have not heard this Esperanto. Maybe I should like to learn it."

"Heard from Lazlo recently?"

"No. My sister says he's been seeing another girl." Her hand took a swipe under one eye, then the other.

"Sorry to hear that. He doesn't know what he's losing."

She smiled.

The bus came and our subject got on board, and we joined the throng. I noticed no one paid and guessed you paid when you got off. Tatty got a seat, and I stood. Our subject was sitting in the middle of the bus. So far he seemed unaware he was being followed. He was plugged into his phone listening to music and looked to be playing a game.

The bus traveled south and we with it. First down LaSalle and then west on 24th. I guessed he probably lived near the lakes. He got off at the Uptown Station and we did too. I asked for transfers when I paid for Tatty and myself. He got on another bus, and we continued our trip south down Hennepin Avenue.

We rode for thirteen blocks until Lonnie got off at 34th Street. We did likewise. He was absorbed in his iPhone world and paid us no attention. Down 34th he walked and when he came to Girard, turned south. We had him. He turned down a walkway I noted the house, and Tatty and I kept walking. We turned around, walked back on the opposite side of the street, and I made note of the house number. I called Tina and reported where we were.

"I'm on my way, Harry. Good work."

Tatty and I walked down to the cemetery and back while waiting for Tina to pick us up.

"So this is what you do when not playing chess," Tatty said.

"Welcome to my world."

"Do you like this work?"

"Yes and no. Can be awfully boring."

"Yes. I can see that. But it does require you to be alert. And when you succeed, it is like saying 'checkmate'."

"Yes, it is. You get a bit of an adrenaline rush."

"Yes."

We were up by 34th Street when Tina arrived in the yellow Crossfire. This was going to be interesting. Three people and two seats. I got in and Tatty squeezed in, sitting on my lap. We got home without mishap. Waiting for us were Logan, Cynice, and Crystal.

Tina invited everyone in and I paid up. They were all happy campers. Two hundred bucks to stand around for two days. Pretty sweet, if you ask me. They thanked us and left.

Tatty lingered momentarily, I suppose hoping I might ask her to stay. Believe me, I was tempted. But what could come from a relationship between Tatty and me? I decided to let her go.

"Where does the birthday boy want to go for dinner?" Tina asked.

"That's right. Today's the day. Hm." I didn't get far in thought when the doorbell rang.

Tina and I looked at each other, and she glanced at her watch.

"I don't think it's Cal," she said. "I don't expect him for another hour."

I went to the door and opened it. Tatty. *What the hell?* I thought. I opened the screen door and let her in. "Is everything all right, Tat?"

She shook her head. "Can we talk?"

"Sure." I led her to the library and closed the door. "What's on your mind?" I asked.

"I don't want you angry with me."

"I'm not."

"I feel you are pushing me away. Blaming me even because we had sex."

"Tat, I'm fifty-two. No. fifty-three. Today's my birthday. You're nineteen. I'm thirty-four years older than you."

"Can we not be friends and enjoy each other?"

"We can."

"Even sex?"

"I suppose. But don't you want more? A husband? Someone your own age? Maybe children? Tat, I'm too old."

"Harry, shouldn't I make that decision?"

I sighed. "What do you want?"

"I want to be your friend. I liked our lovemaking. You're not like the young ones, who are so fast. Can we be that? Friends who sometimes love each other?"

"I don't know, Tatty."

"Let's give it a try. I'm so lonely, Harry."

"All right. We'll give it a try."

"Happy birthday, Harry. And thank you. I feel a lot better. But now I've made you take me home."

"Might as well stay and help me celebrate my birthday."

She hugged me. "I'd like that."

"Me too. Just don't act like my daughter, okay?"

She punched my arm. Then stopped and asked. "Do you have a daughter?"

"No, I don't. But you could be."

"We're buddies. You're not my father. I already have one."

We left the library and found Tina in the living room.

"Hi, Tatty," Tina said. "Decided to help us celebrate Harry's birthday?"

"Yes, Miss Wright."

"Call me, 'Tina'."

The doorbell rang. "That should be Cal," Tina said. "So where to, birthday boy?"

"Gasthof."

"Gasthof, it is."

8

TOLTEC LAND COMPANY

SATURDAY, OCTOBER 13TH

THE FOUR OF us were sitting at the dining room table eating breakfast: Tina, Cal, Tatty, and I. Tina, as usual, was preoccupied with her iPad. Cal was reading the paper, Tatty and I were in the middle of a chess game and, for once, I seemed to be on top. Although I suspected she was letting me win.

The night before, on the way to the Gasthof, I phoned David, and he was available. I told him to begin the surveillance this morning as soon as he could. When we got home from the restaurant, I emailed him the address and photo of the subject.

Cal had been surprised to see Tatty yesterday, but said nothing. The four of us had a wonderful time. In spite of her youth, Tatty can hold her own with a bunch of middle-aged farts. He was even more surprised to see her at breakfast this morning, but again kept any opinions he had to himself.

After breakfast, and another draw, I took Tatty home. She had studying to do. She hugged me, kissed my cheek, and said, "I had a lot of fun, Harry. Thanks. I'm glad we worked things out."

"Me too," I said.

We got out of the car and hugged again. Then she ran up the walk, turned and waved, and disappeared through the front door. I got back in the car and drove home. Cal was still there when I got back. He and Tina were in the living room.

"Harry," Cal began, "it's none of my business, but I'd like to know if you're serious about your young friend."

I laughed. "You find my relationship shocking?"

"Well, yeah, kind of."

"Tatty and I are friends. Have been for a long time. We play chess together online. That's how we met. Then she came here to go to the U. The other night, well, let's just say our relationship went to another level. I doubt it will last, but..." I left it hanging and shrugged.

"Okay." He gave Tina a kiss and announced he had to get home. He had things to do. Tina walked him to the door and then came back to the living room.

"I'm going to spell David so he can take a break," I said.

"I'm sure David will appreciate it. Thanks."

"Catch you later."

I phoned David and told him I was coming. I parked the next block over, walked down the street, back up the alley, and then met David a couple houses north of Lonnie Johnson's house.

"All quiet," David said.

"We're going to need someone to watch the alley," I said.

"True. I did mount a very small remote camera to at least give us a heads up when they leave the garage. Works in real time as well as records."

"Really?"

"Yep. The recording goes to the cloud."

"Okay. You take a break."

David gave me the code so I could watch the garage via the camera on my cell. He then left to take care of business.

Surveillance in a residential neighborhood is on the difficult side. If you leave your car too long, people will call the police. If you sit in your car too long, people will call the police. If they see you walking around for too long, they'll call the police. You have to shake up the routine continually because anything out of the ordinary someone will notice and you'll be explaining what you're doing to the police.

I walked up and down the street, sometimes briskly, sometimes slowly. Sometimes I took my hat off, sometimes my sunglasses. I turned my jacket inside out, then right side out, and even took it off.

When David returned, I got into my car and drove around the block and parked a couple doors down from Brother Leonard's address.

Along about half-past eleven, the remote revealed the garage door opening and a bright orange BMW X1 pulled out.

I started the car, drove down the street, and up the alley. The Beemer was ahead of me, waiting to turn onto 34th. I got a picture of the license plate with my phone. The car drove west, and I attempted to follow.

By the time I got onto 34th, the orange X1 was at the corner of Hennepin. The vehicle turned north, and I did too. Four cars were ahead of me and then I got stuck at a light.

When the light turned green, I attempted to follow, but the big orange crossover was gone.

I drove back to Brother Leonard's house. And so the day went. David and I changing places. Watching, watching, and more watching. Tina came and spelled us for a while, which helped.

Along about three in the afternoon, the orange BMW returned. Didn't get to see who was driving it, however. I called Cal and got him on the third ring.

"Hey, Major."

"Hey, Cal. Say, can you get us an owner for this license plate? And can you get a vehicle for Leonard Johnson at—" I gave him the address.

"This is the guy you think's involved with your missing person?"

"Yes."

"Okay. I'll see what I can find out."

He called me back an hour later. "Hey, Major. The license plate — on an orange BMW?"

"That's the one."

"Is registered to the Toltec Land Company."

"Really? Interesting. Anything on Johnson?"

"Nope. Did run the Toltec Land Company. They own the BMW, a Toyota FJ Cruiser, and a Dodge Caravan."

"Thanks, Cal. Very helpful. Now we know what to look for."

The call ended, and I did a web search for the Toltec Land Company. No website. No info about the company. I checked the Better Business Bureau. Nothing. I checked the Secretary of State's business search. Jackpot. The Toltec Land Company is a corporation. Registered office address? Right here on Girard. Chief Executive Officer was listed as Marguerita Maria Guadalupe Delgado Espinoza and her address was right here, the house we were watching.

Now at this humble address on Girard Avenue South, we had the business address for the Toltec Land Company and the residence of Leonard Harrison Johnson and his wife or girlfriend, the above mentioned Marguerita Delgado Espinoza. As they say, the plot thickens.

What was a puzzlement for me was why a land company in this day and age would have no web presence. I thought it highly unusual. The company had to be making some kind of money to buy over ninety thousand dollars worth of vehicles.

Unless human services workers make more money than your ordinary low-level bureaucrat. And my gut said no.

In addition to this odd mix, Leonard Harrison Johnson was a caver. Did his spelunking interest connect somehow with Toltec Land Company? Probably not, but we didn't know they didn't.

David and I called it a night at eight. All quiet at the Johnson-Delgado Espinoza residence. When I got home Tina had tea and a light supper waiting for me. I took it to the office because Tina doesn't like to talk business outside of the office.

"Thanks a lot, Sis. Really appreciate it." I sat down to eat and reported what I'd discovered.

She leaned back in her custom made ergonomically correct chair and absorbed what I told her. After a bit, she said, "I called Gwen and asked for an update. She said she's been focusing on Osgood. Three days of searching and watching and the guy is squeaky clean. Church member and deacon. Baptist. He doesn't go to movies or bowling or dancing or bars. Not especially well liked at the corporate office, but appears to be as honest as the solar system is wide."

"If he's honest, why isn't he liked?"

"A bit arrogant, self-righteous, self-important. The only flaw in the fabric is his dislike of Edmund. And it might not be specifically a dislike of Edmund, but of college graduates in general. From what Gwen has gathered, he'd make the John Birch Society look liberal."

"Huh. That's a statement."

"Isn't it, though? Anyway, we can't pin anything on Osgood at this point. I asked Gwen to probe if he might have encouraged Edmund Lowell to leave the company."

I shrugged. "Personally I don't see how this will help us."

"Might not. But it might. Won't know until we've finished plowing the field."

I finished my supper and poured myself a cup of tea. Tina lit a cigar and poured herself a glass of madeira. A fire crackled in the fireplace.

"When's Gwen going to check on Lowell?" I asked.

"She isn't sure. Possibly sooner over later since nothing is happening with the investigation of Osgood."

I nodded and drank tea. On a fluke, I keyed in the code and checked the camera focused on Johnson's and Delgado Espinoza's garage, although I suppose officially it would be the Toltec Land Company's garage, and there, at quarter to ten, taillights. I watched the Toyota FJ Cruiser back out.

"Well, I'll be…"

"What is it, Harry?"

"Our subject is going out. Hasn't ventured out all day and at quarter to ten he's going out."

"Maybe he and the Missus are going to party hardy."

"Maybe. Damn, we should've been there."

"We need more bodies and until we have them, opportunities will pass us by. That's just how it is. A twenty-four-hour surveillance takes a lot of people. You know that."

"But that's what we need if we're going to do this right."

"Or a little bit of luck."

"Yeah, that would help."

"I don't know why you're all bent out of shape over this. I'm the detective. You're the grunt."

"Yeah. You're right. Great. I'm not worrying about it. And on that note, I'm going to bed."

"I'll spell you and David tomorrow."

"Thanks."

I fell asleep thinking teaching college was a whole lot more rewarding than what I was doing at the moment.

9

NICOLLET ISLAND
SUNDAY, OCTOBER 14TH

I SHOWED up at our surveillance site a little after ten. David was glad to see me; he needed a break. Bundled up for winter, I walked up the street and down the street. I walked up the alley and down the alley. After which, I sat in the car. I started the engine to get a little heat going when I noticed the garage door opening. Out backed the orange BMW, which drove down the alley, heading north. And, as these things go, I was facing south.

I put the car in gear, drove to the end of the block (Girard is a one way, heading south), made two lefts, and was cruising up the alley. I watched the crossover turn left and gave my car gas.

At 34th, checked traffic, gunned it, pulling out ahead of a Toyota, and just missed getting broadsided. I shot down the street, watched the BMW turn right onto Hennepin, gunned it around the corner on a yellow light.

My quarry was half a block ahead of me. Not wanting to get stuck at a light, I closed the distance. Only to have a little Kia pull out in front of me. I hit the brakes, swerved into the left lane, and got around the car. That was a close call.

The BMW was now two car lengths ahead of me. The light changed from green to yellow. I watched it cruise through the intersection. I tramped on the accelerator, and my Focus followed as the light turned red. I prayed for no cops to be around and no flashing lights appeared. Definite proof God answers prayer.

I caught up with the orange crossover at the next light. A woman was driving. Must be Marguerita Maria Guadalupe Delgado Espinoza. I had sunglasses on. I pulled my hat down to cover my face a little more.

The light turned green, and we continued down Hennepin, when, without warning, she pulled into an open space on the side of the street. There was nothing I could do but drive on and make a right turn on the next street, drive around the block and come out at Hennepin.

At the corner I looked in both directions. Nothing. I'd been made. Damn it anyway. I sent a text to David explaining in brief what happened and that I was heading home to get a different vehicle.

Tina has a Ford Flex which she rarely uses. She doesn't like it. Her favorite car is her Alfa Romeo. An antique to be sure: a 1969 Spider Veloce. Because of its age, she hardly ever drives it. Her everyday cars are her Ford Thunderbird and Chrysler Crossfire. The problem with them, as I see it, is that they're two-seaters. There is nothing wrong with the Flex. It merely seats more than two.

When I got home, I told Tina what happened.

"Don't worry about it, Harry. She only connected with the vehicle. She doesn't know the scale of the operation. But I'm changing up the assignments."

"Why?"

"One of the databases I checked, revealed a total of four properties owned by Toltec in Minneapolis."

"Really?"

"Yep. I confirmed ownership with Property Tax Information. The house on Girard and an apartment building on Girard. A house on Nicollet Island and a commercial property on Lake. They may own more, but we'll start there. Tell David what I've told you and let him know you will conduct the stake out of the property on Nicollet Island. He can keep his eye on the apartment building as well as the house on Girard." She passed me a sheet of paper. "Those are the addresses."

"Sounds good. I'm taking the Flex."

"Be my guest. Tell David I'll be by to spell him."

"Will do."

I phoned David while getting into the Flex and conveyed the information Tina had found to him, along with my surveillance change.

"Thanks, Harry. Too bad about getting caught. Happens to all of us."

"It does," I replied. "Catch you later."

I drove over to Nicollet Island. Despite living in Minnesota and around or in Minneapolis for a big chunk of my life, I was on Nicollet Island but once. The time I ate dinner at the Nicollet Island Inn. Now I get to conduct surveillance on the island. An adventure within an adventure.

The address was easy to find. I didn't even need GPS. Parked in front was an orange BMW with a license plate number near and dear to my heart.

Nothing is secret anymore. Privacy is an illusion. Our lives are open books to whoever has the access to the technology to lay our souls bare and naked before the prying eyes of anyone who wishes to pry.

I drove on past the house and around the block and past the place again. Turning the corner, I parked, after positioning the Flex so I could observe if the BMW drove by the cross street I was on.

All was quiet and after fifteen minutes I got out and walked down the street, taking a good look at the house on my way to the next intersection.

You might wonder why I didn't simply slap a GPS tracker on the car, go home, and monitor its movements. Because I certainly could have. To do so would be a lot easier than what I was doing. And believe you me, I was very much tempted.

Unfortunately, while our lives might be open books, it is illegal for me to violate a person's expectation of privacy in his or her vehicle. The state may control everything about that vehicle from registering it, to licensing it, to taxing it, to controlling if it can even be driven (read, is it street legal or properly insured), but you and I still have a right to privacy in that vehicle.

Consequently, I could put a tracking device on the car, but to do so would be illegal without the owner's consent. Let's hear it for our right to privacy.

I kept an eye on the house and car for three hours. Then, having moved my vehicle to a different location, I watched a woman, a very beautiful woman, if the binoculars weren't lying to me, leave the house and get into the orange BMW. She drove past me and I gave her fifteen seconds before I pulled away from the curb and followed her all the way back to south Minneapolis.

David was waiting for me and signaled for us to talk, I parked around the corner and met him.

"Hey, Harry. Nothing going on here. Tina said to break it off. Anything happen on the island?"

"Not that I could see. I'm going to need an upgrade on my x-ray vision."

"You do that. Anyway, Tina said she's rethinking this. I'm heading home."

"Okay, David. Send me your report and I'll send out a check."

"Thanks. Catch you later."

I drove on home. Tina had tea ready and had actually cooked a pot roast in the crock pot. She'd waited for me, so we ate together and shared a bottle of Leon Millot. Then we retired to the office.

"David said you're rethinking things."

She lit a cigar and poured herself a glass of Malmsey madeira. I decided a port would be nice and a pipe as well. When I hauled out the pipe, she said, "You aren't smoking that latakia shit."

I shook my head and said, "Virginia."

"Yes, I'm rethinking things. Gwen emailed. She's shifting to Lowell. She's convinced Osgood didn't like Edmund and didn't want him to take over the company. But that appears to be the extent of it. He doesn't appear to have had any contact in the past two years with the younger Lowell, nor does it seem he was instrumental in him leaving. Osgood appears to be a dead end."

"There is the elder Lowell."

"There is. And he appears more likely in my mind. But we'll see. For now, I will find out if I can't persuade Brother Leonard to tell me more about his operation."

"He was pretty tight-lipped."

"He was. But I'm going to see if I can't loosen those lips and sink a few ships."

"Good luck with that."

"You don't think I can?"

"Didn't say that. But you didn't see the woman I saw. If

that was Marguerita, you better hope she's hell to live with because she'd make the Venus de Milo weep with envy."

"Huh. You don't think I can seduce a man and still keep the store locked? Huh. My own brother doubts me. Fine. Be that way. We'll find out."

I rolled my eyes. "I'm doubting nothing. I'm not saying you can't climb the Matterhorn. I'm simply saying you might be underestimating the difficulty. But if you don't want to listen to me, then suffer. What can I say?"

Nearly twenty pounds of Maine Coon cat jumped onto my lap.

"Prudy's missed you," Tina said, and added, "A word to the wise is sufficient."

I finished my port and my pipe, said, "Thank you," and refilled the glass.

Tina continued. "A young man graduates from college. He's being groomed to take over the family business. He is heir to a very nice pile of money. By all accounts, he was doing well at learning the ropes. Then one day an argument with his father sets him off, and he leaves. Why that particular argument? Why was it different from the others? Maybe it wasn't. Maybe new information made what was a normal occurrence something out of the ordinary.

"In any event, he leaves. He travels for two years, ends up in Minneapolis. Here, he's beaten and robbed and then meets Brother Leonard and promptly disappears. Don't you think that odd, Harry? He's already spent most of the past two years out West. Why would he want to go back there and work? He wanted to go home. Why go back West?"

"He needed money."

"He had access to the piles of money his father had made." Tina blew smoke towards the ceiling.

"Perhaps. But then he didn't necessarily even need to go west to get money. He could work day labor here or panhandle and get enough for a bus ticket home. Hell, the welfare department might even pay for a bus ticket to send him elsewhere."

"True. But, as I said, he meets Brother Leonard and disappears. Then we look at Brother Leonard. A do-gooder welfare worker helping the poor and homeless get jobs out of state. Why out of state? Why not here?"

"Maybe he's like most liberal snobs and gives lip service to helping the problem while all along he just shoves it under the rug or throws a little money at it. The welfare system wasn't really designed to help people. It was designed to make people dependent on a certain political party. Vote buying. If it was meant to help them, it would be designed to succeed. To put itself out of business, instead of enabling people and keeping them in poverty."

"Harry, you are on your soapbox again."

"I am. Sorry. But that just might be his solution. Move the homeless problem out of state to some other state."

"Perhaps. I wonder if we can get a number on just how many people Brother Leonard has helped?"

"We can ask. Want me to tackle that tomorrow?"

"Sure. I'd like to have an idea from someone other than Brother Leonard."

"Okay. I'll talk to folks tomorrow and see what I can find out."

"Then, after finding out about Brother Leonard, we go on to discover he doesn't seem to own anything. Everything is owned by the Toltec Land Company, which is run by the mysterious Marguerita Maria Guadalupe Delgado Espinoza."

"She's mysterious?"

Tina nodded and blew out a cloud of smoke. "Very. She

doesn't show up anywhere. It's as though she doesn't really exist."

"Maybe she doesn't."

"Or she keeps way under the radar for some reason."

"Might be here illegally."

"Possible. Except, according to the current administration and other folks in Washington, no one is truly illegal. They're all citizen's, just on the wrong side of an antiquated law."

I laughed. "You sound like me."

"Goodness. I'd best keep my distance." She puffed on her cigar. "That's where we are."

"Other than discovering Brother Leonard, we aren't very far along."

"We've also ruled out any involvement by Osgood." Tina sighed.

"So no hit man hired by Osgood to take out young Lowell and thereby assure Osgood's ascension to the throne?"

"No. No hit man. At least as far as I can see. But I might check with someone at the Bureau."

"Good grief."

"Just because I haven't found a connection — actually Gwen hasn't found a connection—"

"Don't go passing the buck."

She cleared her throat. "Just because no connection has been found, doesn't mean one doesn't exist."

"If you say so. I'm hitting the hay. I'm tired. See you in the morning."

I gave her a kiss on the cheek and left her formulating conspiracy theories worthy of spy novel plots.

10

SATAN'S CAVE

MONDAY, OCTOBER 15TH

EARLY IN THE MORNING, Ed called and asked if we had any work for him. I told him not at the moment. We'd taken care of what we needed to on the weekend.

During the day, I spent my time catching up on report writing and the submission of a few final bills. I'd been holding off in part to make sure the attorneys were done with our services. I got David's report and timesheet and wrote him a check for his weekend work.

A private investigator provides services for a fee. Consequently, the work of a private investigator can be seen in two parts: providing a service someone needs or wants done and the collection of the fee to provide said service. Often enough, once the service has been performed, the collection of the fee becomes an onerous chore with the client who couldn't live without you suddenly wondering who you are and what do you want.

More than once, Tina's had to threaten legal action to get a recalcitrant client to pay up. And one time, when we did go to court, the person ended up declaring bankruptcy and Wright

Investigations got stiffed out of $5,329. I do my best to keep on top of billing and report writing. We don't want to waste the warm afterglow of success.

I took a break from writing reports and billing clients to make grilled vegetable sandwiches for lunch. The veggies had been tenderizing for three hours or a little more. I grilled enough vegetables and toasted enough baguettes to make four sandwiches. I opened a lovely Gewürztraminer to have with the meal and told Tina to come and get them. I also put on some Bantock to play through the sound system.

Tina doesn't like to talk about business while eating and today was no different.

"Everything okay with Tatiana?" she asked.

"As far as I know."

"She's really into spelunking? This is very good, by the way."

"Thanks. I guess so. She's a geology major, so makes sense."

"Some people climb mountains. Some burrow in the earth."

"True. I guess she'd rather explore underground."

The conversation meandered to a variety of other topics, none of which I can now remember. When lunch was over, I went back to the reports and billing and Tina went back to reading a book on interviewing techniques. By mid-afternoon I was done and moved to the kitchen to prepare supper. I was making a polenta pie with Gorgonzola and a mixed green salad. Perhaps a Fume Blanc to go with the pie.

In the middle of making the salad, my phone chimed. I wiped my hands and checked. A text from Tatty.

Want to go urban spelunking tonight?

> Thanks for asking, but unfortunately I'm working.

Damn. Supper?

> Come over. Polenta pie.

There was a long pause; then,

I'll be there ASAP.

Almost an hour later the doorbell rang and Tatty was the one ringing.

"Hi, Harry."

"Hi, Tat." I motioned for her to come in. She gave me a hug. "How did you get here?" I asked.

"Bus."

I took her coat. She was dressed in old clothes and laughed when I looked at her.

"Caving clothes."

"I guess," I replied with a smile. "C'mon. We're ready to eat."

"Good. I'm starving. Thanks for inviting me."

"My pleasure." I put my arm around her and walked her to the dining room. "Have a seat. Tina will be here any second. I'll get the food."

I brought out the pie, then back to the kitchen for the salad, and finally the wine.

Tina was there by then, chatting with Tatty. I poured wine and told the ladies to help themselves.

"Where are these caves?" Tina asked.

"Oh, all over," my friend replied. "There's one under downtown. It is very difficult to get to."

"Minneapolis?" Tina asked.

"Yes, Minneapolis. Lots of them along the river. Both natural and manmade. There are old basements and sub-basements, tunnels, many underground structures exist. Some have had their entrances covered up, but they are still there. The Ford company when it demolishes the factory along the river will fill in the shallow tunnels. The deep ones they'll seal off, but they will still be there."

"Interesting."

"Tonight we're going to Nicollet Island and explore Satan's Cave."

"Nicollet Island?" I said.

"Yes. The rumor is there are five caves under the island. But only two have been found. Satan's and Santa's. I think beer was aged in them in the nineteenth century. I'm looking forward to the adventure."

"That's very interesting, Tatty," Tina said. "Do you take pictures?"

"Sometimes I do. In this group, Logan is the person who likes to take pictures. If I take one, it is usually with my cell phone."

"How do you enter these places?" Tina asked.

"It depends on what it is. Often you have to enter through the sewer system and that is easiest done through a manhole. Just remove the cover and climb down."

"Is it that easy to remove a manhole cover?" I asked.

"They are heavy. It helps to have a hook and two people to do the lifting. Logan is very serious. He has a very fancy tool for removing manhole covers. It cost him over a thousand dollars."

I raised my eyebrows. "I guess he is serious."

"Very serious."

"Let me know how your adventure goes tonight," I said.

"You sure you don't want to come along?"

"I'm working."

"How late?"

"I don't know. Probably be done by nine or ten."

"We aren't starting until eleven. Want to make sure most people are indoors for the night. You sure you don't want to go caving with me?"

Tina had a big grin on her face.

"If I get done in time, I'll go."

Now Tatty had a big grin on her face and Tina said, "Just don't get caught."

"This is safer than the U tunnels," Tat assured her.

We finished eating, and I drove Tat back to her place and then drove on to the men's shelters to see if I could get more information on Brother Leonard's activities. I can't say the information I got was all that helpful. On the other hand, it was more helpful than falling down a flight of stairs. The information ranged from, "Brother Who?" to "He's of the devil. No good comes out of dealing with him." Which is about as broad a range of replies as one can get. A couple of the more helpful ones were:

In the past year? Oh, I'd say he's probably been to this shelter four times. Each time he gets a few volunteers. How many? Well, I'm not sure. Never counted. Hey, Wendell, how many guys would you say took Brother Leonard up on his offer of housing and work? Twelve to fifteen? In the past year? Well, there you have it. Twelve to fifteen. Have any of them ever come back? No. Can't say I've seen any come back who went off with him. Hey, Wendell, any of those guys ever come back here? No? Nope. None of 'em ever came back. Do I think that strange? Well, I dunno. If they got themselves three hots and a cot and a job to boot, no, I don't think it strange. Did I know Edmund Lowell? No. Name doesn't ring a bell.

And:

He drives up in that black Dodge Caravan. He himself wears a black suit. But he's all smiles and friendly. Doing the Lord's work. Trying to find men who want work and a place to live. Most aren't interested. They have to get sober or quit using. But a few take him up on his offer. Yep. Out west. Always a place out west. Do I think that odd? No. Guess not. It's where his friend is who can use the workers. How many in the past year? At our shelter? Maybe six. Eight. I don't keep count. How do they get out west? Beats me. I'd guess by bus. But that's just a guess. Lowell? Edmund Lowell? No. Yeah. That picture looks a little familiar. But we see lots of guys here.

The most helpful was an old man who told me he and Edmund met at the shelter and stayed under the bridge for a few nights. "But the boy wasn't well," the old guy said. "So's I got him back here and it jus' so happens Brother Leonard was visiting. He saw the boy wasn't doin' good. So's he says, 'What's your name?' And the boy says 'Edmund'. 'Well, Edmund, tell you what I'm gonna do. I'll take you home and get you well and then get you a job.' The young fella says, 'I don't need no job, Mister. I jes need to get home.' And Brother Leonard, he says, 'Well, Edmund, we'll get you well and get you home.' And so's the young fella he goes off with Brother Leonard and that's that. Haven't seen 'im since. Brother

Leonard musta sent him home. Boy wasn't sick enough to die. But then you never know." I asked him when that was. He said, "July fourth."

That was probably the most detailed information we were going to get. I wrote it up and asked the old guy to sign and date it. "For his parents," I said. The guy nodded and signed and dated what I wrote. With that information in hand, I drove back home and reported to Tina.

"In honor of Nero Wolfe, 'satisfactory'," she said.

I laughed.

Then she added, "Go pick up your girlfriend and check out her cave."

"God, you're gross."

Tina laughed out loud. In fact, doubled up with laughter. Sometimes I think she is a bit obsessed with the actions that lead to human reproduction.

I texted Tatty, and she said I was welcome to come over. I told Tina I was off on my spelunking adventure and left for Tat's place.

———

Eleven o'clock found Logan, Cynice, Tatty, and yours truly on Nicollet Island.

"Good to see you again, Harry," Logan said, while shaking my hand.

"Yeah, Harry, good to see you," Cynice said, giving me a hug. I caught a whiff of weed clinging to her hair and clothes.

I replied in kind and Logan said, "Let's get started." Once the manhole cover was removed, we climbed down into the hole. Each of the other three carried a small pack. I didn't have a pack. I made do with the cargo pockets on my trousers to store extra batteries and an extra mini-flashlight.

The walls were brick, and a pipe ran along the floor. The corridor wasn't overly wide. With outstretched arms I could easily touch both walls. The bricks were dry and crumbly with age. Sections of the floor were at times covered with muck and walking on the pipe kept our feet out of it.

We walked for quite a while, slowly making our way through the rather monotonous looking maze. The air was warm, so the walking wasn't uncomfortable. I took a couple pictures with my cell.

At last we came to a fissure in the wall and Logan said, "This is it." I took a picture of Tatty going into 'The Beyond'. The four of us ended up in a longish room after we made our way through the crawl space and dropped down to the cave.

There was ample evidence of people having preceded us. Candles. Food wrappers. Beer cans. Even a condom. The walls were sandstone, which gave the cave a dry feel.

Cynice took out of her pack a small bottle of brandy for us to share. Just like my college days. Except then it was a joint that went around the circle.

Logan talked about the other known cave under the island's surface. Why it's called 'Santa's Cave' and this one 'Satan's Cave' he didn't know.

The bottle made three or four rounds and I knew I was beginning to feel a little on the mellow side. Cynice started tickling Logan and pretty soon they had some serious kissing and groping going on.

Tatty looked at me and I looked at her. She's a beautiful young woman who could be my daughter. She isn't, though. And there in that room I don't know how many feet below the surface of the earth, warm, and filled with the sounds of Logan's and Cynice's lovemaking, my inhibitions and restraints numbed by the brandy, I took her hand. She sidled in close to me and we kissed each other and it wasn't long before the sounds of our lovemaking joined those of Logan and Cynice.

When all was quiet, I said, "Is this called spelunking with benefits?" Tatty laughed and Cynice giggled. Logan merely shrugged, but his face held a huge grin. We got ourselves put back together, and I took a selfie of Tatty and I and a picture of Logan and Cynice. A memento of our adventure in Satan's Cave.

Logan led us in a different direction than the one by which we entered the tunnels and the cave. More brick tunnels. Much more muck on the floor than before. We came to a different exit. But neither he nor I could budge the manhole cover. "It happens," he said.

We walked on. "Let's try this one," he said. He got up under it and pushed. It finally popped open. He took a look around and called down, "All quiet topside." And up we went into the chilly night air. Which actually felt pretty good after being in the warm stuffy air of the tunnels.

We walked back to our cars, said good night, and drove off.

"The one thing I don't like is getting the inside of my car mucked up with God knows what," I said.

"You brought plastic bags," Tatty said, "that will help."

"It will. Hopefully anyway. That passage coming out. God. I think my boots are wrecked."

"Don't be a sissy, Harry."

I looked at her. Our eyes met, and we started laughing. She chatted on the drive to her place, the big house she shares with five other young women. I pulled up in front.

She touched my cheek, kissed me, and said, "I'm not so lonely when I'm with you." Her eyes searched my face, and I touched her cheek. Then I leaned in and kissed her.

"Tatty, I—"

Her fingers touched my lips, and she shook her head. "We

are best friends, Harry. And we always will be. Goodnight."
She got out of the car, waved, and ran up the walk.

I watched until she entered the house and then drove home.

Loneliness is a funny thing. Why is it I feel more lonely than ever after I've been with her?

11

FIRED

TUESDAY, OCTOBER 16TH

TINA WAS asleep by the time I got home in the wee hours of the morning. Which probably accounts for her unusual chattiness at breakfast.

"So tell me all about it," she said.

I told her, leaving out those details which would appeal to her prurient interests.

"Doesn't sound overly interesting if you ask me."

"You're right. I think you have to have a certain mindset, have certain tastes and predilections for mucking about in cramped and dark underground places. To be honest, it isn't my highest priority."

"At least you didn't get caught."

"No. I didn't get caught."

"Gwen called last night. She talked with a few people yesterday and asked general questions about senior and junior Lowell and their relationship with each other. Didn't get too far. The people weren't willing to say a whole lot."

"Any particular reason?"

"Gwen thought it was due to her being a non-local."

"Could be."

"She also dug deeper into his finances."

"Whose?"

"Senior Lowell. He's easily worth twenty or thirty million.

"A nice chunk of change."

"It is indeed. Gwen will continue checking today."

"And what do you want me to do?"

"Not sure. I'm going to meet with Lonnie Johnson. Lunch. See if I can get him to open up."

"Good luck with that."

"Yeah, I'll need it."

"When's lunch?"

"Eleven-thirty."

"So that's why you're not in a suit."

"Uh-huh."

She was wearing a tight pair of blue jeans, stiletto heels, a tight emerald green sweater with a V-neckline revealing just enough cleavage to get the imagination going.

Her toast and tea finished, she said, "I'll be in the office."

I cleared off the dining room table. In the kitchen, I put the dishes in the dishwasher and leftover food in the fridge. I poured myself a cup of tea and took it to the office.

Tina was at her desk looking over the statements I'd gotten from the guys I interviewed last night and comparing them with the ones from Ed and Stinky.

"Is he the same guy Stinky interviewed? The guy you got to sign the statement regarding the fourth?"

"Don't know. Didn't ask, and he didn't say if someone else was around asking the same questions."

She nodded and went on reading. I entered time and expenses on our log sheet for the Lowell case and began typing up my notes.

At quarter to eleven, Tina announced she was leaving for her lunch date. I wished her good luck and kept typing. Prudy took over Tina's chair when she left and Isis was snuggled next to her. Where Manly was was anyone's guess. Somewhere in and amongst the score plus ten rooms.

Just after eleven, the phone rang. I answered, "Wright Investigations."

The voice on the other end yelled, "What the hell do you think you're doing?"

"Typing," I replied.

The voice paused. My guess was I'd caught him off guard and he didn't have a handy comeback. Then I heard, "I want to speak with Miss Wright."

"She's not available at the moment. I'm Harry Wright, her assistant. May I help you?"

"This is Ralph Lowell. I want to know what the hell you are doing spending my money investigating me?"

"Miss Wright is checking out possible clues to your son's disappearance that she didn't think you were forthright in giving her."

"Such as?"

"Why your son up and quit in the first place."

"Whatever happened here has no bearing on his disappearing there. You're wasting my money and time."

"Miss Wright is apparently of a different opinion. She's the boss and I'm the water boy."

"Well, Mr. Water Boy, you tell your boss she's fired. I'm terminating the contract as of right now. I want an itemized list of expenses and a refund of all expenses related to your investigation of me and if I don't get it — I'll sue your ass. Do I make myself clear?"

"You did."

"Good." And he hung up.

I sighed and put the phone back on the cradle. I thought a minute and texted Gwen:

> Got caught. Suspend operation until further
> notice.

After a couple minutes, she texted back:

> Damn. Was afraid word might get back to
> Lowell. Sorry.

Don't worry. This is the case on which we're
all getting caught.

Next I texted Tina:

Caught. We're fired.

After a minute:

> Damn. Will go through with lunch.

I started tallying up the expenses incurred to this point.
Tina's lunch wouldn't count, but I would expense the drive
downtown. Gwen hadn't totaled up her time yet, which,
depending on Tina's mood, we may or may not charge him for.
She may say, "Let him sue us."

Twelve-thirty I took a lunch break. Microwaved a few leftovers, and took the food back to my desk. Getting fired has
only happened twice since I've been with Tina. Not something
I'm used to. I don't think Tina is either. Due to the hefty
retainer, we'll at least get the money we earned. I was just
about finished with my meal when Tina came into the office.
The look on her face told me we'd just had three strikes.

She sat at her desk, poured herself a glass of madeira,
drank half of it, and lit a cigar. She glowered at me.

"I don't think it's my fault," I said.

"No, it's not," she growled.

"Did he break up with you?"

She gave me a disgusted look. "The bastard took my picture, did an image search, and found out I was a detective."

"So much for the southern drawl."

"Yeah, right."

"So what did he say?"

"We met. I even gave him a little hug. He smiled. We sat, and he said, 'How long shall we play this charade, Justinia Wright?' I didn't try to bullshit my way through. I just said, 'How did you find out?' He said, 'Reversed image search.' I nodded. He then asked what it was all about. I told him. He said Edmund had some sort of stomach bug, he got over it, and he sent him home. If he didn't get there, he had no control over that."

"You think he's telling the truth?"

"I don't know. I kind of doubt it. He's too cagey and suspicious. Like he has something he wants to keep hidden."

"So what did he do with Edmund Lowell? What does he do with all the homeless guys?"

"That is the question, isn't it? And I guess I won't find out since we got fired."

I told her what Ralph Lowell had said to me.

"Tell Gwen to come home. I'm going to tickle the ivories." She downed the rest of the madeira in the glass and with her cigar, left the office.

I texted Gwen to catch the next flight home and got back to work on the expense report. At five, I knocked off and headed for the kitchen to make supper. Since Tina and I both love Italian and because we got fired and her ruse was busted, I decided to make comfort food. For us, that is pasta e fagioli. By six the soupy stew was ready. I walked over to the music room and told her the grub was on the table.

She was really in a funk because she said but two words the entire meal: thank you. She also had two glasses of chianti. When finished eating, she helped me clean up, filled a bowl with frozen custard, added half a bottle of maraschino cherries, and took it to the living room where she built a fire in the fireplace and ate the custard while watching the flames.

I left her alone. Nothing I'd say would cheer her up. I camped out in the library listening to Bantock symphonies and smoking my pipe. Around ten she went to bed. Gwen texted shortly after saying she'd be in Minneapolis at eight-twenty tomorrow morning and would I pick her up at the airport. I texted back I would.

At quarter to eleven I checked my email and saw one from Mrs. Lowell. It read:

Please disregard my husband's action earlier today. You are still very much on the case. Thank you for your hard work in trying to find Edmund. I appreciate all you are doing.

Very interesting. Now we were going to get caught up between the dueling Lowells. Maybe it would be best to let Mrs. Lowell know what Lonnie Johnson had said and let it go at that. In any case, we should probably wash our hands of the case.

I texted Tatty and asked if she wanted to come over. Her reply informed me she was studying for a test and wouldn't get any studying done if she came over. She signed off, "Szeretlek. T." I had to look the word up and when I did, I was surprised. My chess buddy had just told me she loved me.

Tatty's a beautiful young woman and I enjoy being with her. But she is nineteen. No matter what goes on between us, she is too young. Right now I might not be too old for her, but in twenty or twenty-five years? I have a Benjamin that says she'll want someone her own age.

Probably a good thing she wasn't available. Now I'll go to bed and get some sleep and in the morning tell Tina the Lowells are trying to decide if we're fired or not. My money? It's on Mrs. Lowell.

12

HALLOWEEN GAMBIT

WEDNESDAY, OCTOBER 17TH

THE SKY WAS OVERCAST, with the wind blowing out of the southeast at fifteen miles per hour and gusting to twenty. The temperature was fifty-six, but didn't feel like it one bit. A perfectly nice day to sit by the fire and read a book. But that wasn't happening.

I made tea, put the pot on the warmer, and grabbed a quick cup along with toast and a soft-boiled egg before I raced off to the airport to pick up Gwen.

On the way back, we talked a bit about what she did in Ohio, where she thought she might have screwed up, and that she'd be by later with her activities and expense reports. I dropped her off at her place and turned the nose of the car towards the pile on West Franklin that I call home.

When I walked into the little mansion, I didn't see Tina anywhere obvious, but I wasn't going to check all thirty rooms. It was clear she'd not shown up for breakfast. She was in a blue rain funk all right. I think what got her is the guy she wanted to outfox, outfoxed her.

Technology and I get along, although I'm certainly no whiz kid at it. In truth, I don't care to be — anymore than I'd care to be a mechanic in order to drive my car. Tina, though, at least likes to think she's up on all the latest tech toys. For her, our subject's coup hit her right where it hurt the most — her pride.

I took tea to the office and started a fire in the fireplace. One might think finding firewood in the city difficult. Actually, it is quite easy. There are so many trees in the city and when they come down due to storms or ice or construction one can easily get cord upon cord of firewood. All you need is a chainsaw and a means to haul the wood. Right at this moment we keep a cord of firewood at the house and have five cords in storage facilities. Yes, Tina pays storage fees just so we can have plenty of firewood available.

With a cheery fire going in the office fireplace, I sat at my desk drinking tea and working on the report and expenses for Lowell. In the morning email, a note from Ralph Lowell told us to disregard Vera's email. We were still fired. An hour later another email showed up from Vera Lowell telling us to disregard Ralph. We were unfired and were to keep working on finding her son. Fifteen minutes later another email from Ralph told us, if Vera had sent another email, to just delete it. We were fired and weren't to continue the investigation.

The joys of marriage. Surely it's an institution designed for two people to be bound together in misery and hopefully pass that misery onto the offspring they are supposed to produce. Thank goodness no offspring were produced from my marriage.

Tina showed up just before lunch. She sat at her desk and asked if there was anything new. I told her the Lowells couldn't decide if we were fired or not. She rolled her eyes and shook her head. Then lit a cigar and poured a glass of madeira.

"Have you had anything to eat?"

She shook her head.

This called for intervention, and I relocated to the kitchen.

With toast and a soft-boiled egg prepared, I returned to the office, and sat the plate on her desk.

"Eat this," I commanded, "before you start soaking up the madeira."

She looked at the plate, looked at me, and a smile touched her lips. "Okay, big brother."

When she'd eaten, I took the plate away and returned it to the kitchen. I came back to the office with a cup of tea for her. She took a sip. "I love you, Harry. Thanks."

"Love you, too."

I returned to the kitchen, fixed myself lunch, and brought it back to the office. Tina was sitting by the fire drinking her tea. I sat with her and ate my food.

Her eyes were focused on the flames. She said, "It's them. I can't prove it, but they're doing something to these homeless men they take in. And now we've been fired. But worse, we've been compromised."

"I have a Benjamin riding on Mrs. Lowell to win."

Tina gave me a sidelong glance. "With whom?"

"Myself."

She laughed. "Okay."

"We need to plan how to break open the coconut, so we're ready when Ralph tips his king over."

She stared at the fire and drank tea until her cup was empty. She looked at me and said, "If we can't work secretly, then we'll work openly."

"Certainly makes things simpler."

"I also want a total count if we can get it, year by year, of the number of homeless our dear Brother Leonard has 'helped'. Best to put Ed and Stinky on that project."

"Do we start this now or wait until the Lowells figure out what they're doing?"

"We'll give the Lowells one more day."

"Okay. Then what?"

"We call them and get them both on the same page. And hopefully it's the page for us to continue."

"Really?"

"Yes. Really. I want to find out what Lonnie and Margie are up to. Because my gut says it's no good."

"And of course you want to get paid for finding out."

"Of course. People don't eat on the performance of good deeds."

"No. They don't. The grocery store is a stickler for money."

"That they are." She stood. "Thanks, Harry. I'm going to play the piano for a while."

"All right. Gwen's coming over sometime to give you her report and me her expense sheet."

"Tell her to wait until we find out about the Lowells first."

"Will do."

Tina left, and I called Gwen and told her to hold off on giving Tina her report because we might be back on the job.

"You're kidding me. Really?"

"I'm not and, yes, really."

I could sense her shrug through the phone. "Okay," she said, "keep me posted."

"Will do."

Phone call made, I returned to writing up the Lowell report. If we picked up the case again, at least I'd have everything current. And it's nice to have the paperwork current. I hate playing catch up.

At four-thirty I called it a day. For supper, I decided to make mac and cheese and a tossed salad of mixed greens and a variety of veggies. I was right in the middle when the phone rang. I wiped my hands and answered it.

"Hello, Harry!"

"Hi, Tatty. Test go well?"

"It did. Are you busy tonight?"

"Not really."

"Do you want to hang out?"

"Sure. Are you free to stop by for supper?"

"Yes! I'd like very much to eat with you."

"Do you need a ride?"

"I'll catch the bus. I'll be there as soon as I can."

"Okay. I'll wait for you."

"See you!"

I hung up and returned to the meal preparation. A pleasant surprise to have Tatty coming over. I wiped my hands again and walked to the music room. Tina was playing piano music by Amy Beach.

"Tatty's coming over for supper."

"Okay. Do you want me around?"

"You live here."

"Thanks."

I returned to the kitchen. By quarter to six everything was done. We just needed Tatty.

Tina came out to the dining room, and I poured us each a glass of Riesling. Of course the doorbell rang before the first sip. I answered and there was Tat. I invited her in and took her coat. She was dressed in blue jeans and a dark red blouse with long sleeves. I led her to the dining room and poured her a glass of wine.

We drank and nibbled on the appetizers. I'd made three kinds: cucumber slices topped with whipped feta, basil, and sun-dried tomatoes; Paula Deen's mushroom canapés; and crostinis topped with chickpeas, pimento, and garlic mayo.

When our wine was gone, I brought out the salad, mac and cheese, and a pinot noir.

"How's your case progressing?" Tatty asked.

"We got fired," I said.

"But the husband and wife aren't in agreement. We might be back on the job," Tina said.

"That is good? To be not fired?" Tatty asked.

"Very good," I said.

"You exploring more caves?" Tina asked.

"We're planning on Saturday night," Tatty said.

"Where?" I asked.

"Nicollet Island again. Want to come with us?"

"Hopefully I'll be working. I'll let you know."

"I hope you can make it," Tatty said.

I gave her a smile. "We'll see."

The conversation drifted to other subjects and when supper was over, Tatty helped me clean up. Kitchen duties completed, she and I went to the game room and played chess.

Our first game I drew white and opened e4. She replied e5 and in two more moves we were playing the placid Four Knight's Game. I figured what the heck and played Nxe5 for my fourth move. The very risky Halloween Gambit.

Tatty lifted her eyes from the board and met mine. "You will lose your knight. Is this a mistake?"

"Nope. The Halloween Gambit."

"This is not a joke?"

"Nope. I think the move was first played by Oscar Cordel."

"This is new to me."

"Ha! Have fun." I flashed her a wicked smile.

She took the knight, and the game began in earnest. The violent nature of my attack had Tatty on the defensive and her play was uncharacteristically hesitant. By move twenty-eight she was in hot water and a mere four moves later her ship was taking on water fast.

"Harry, this is a devilish opening. I understand the name."

"It is indeed."

"I am lost, my friend. You win. A very good game."

"Thanks." I was bursting inside, but I didn't want to jump up and down screaming I'd just beaten Tatiana Bogar FIDE Woman Master. After all, she was my guest and that would've been just plain rude.

"We will play another game," she said.

And we did. I played my usual Owen's Defense and held Tatty to a draw.

"Tonight is your night, Harry. Congratulations. Enough chess."

"What? When I'm finally winning?"

Her laugh was deep and throaty. "I think you'd rather make love to me. No?"

"Really? You'd rather screw around instead of playing chess?"

"It is a sacrifice I'm willing to make."

A glorious night it was. I beat Tatty at chess and didn't have to sleep alone. Life can be downright delicious.

13

WORKING

THURSDAY, OCTOBER 18TH

SINCE TATTY HAD AN EARLY CLASS, I had her to her place by half-past six. She showered and dressed within thirty-five minutes. We then swung by Panera and grabbed breakfast. A cheese pastry, orange scone, and cappuccino for Tatty. Two cinnamon crunch and two orange scones for moi, plus hot tea. We ate while I drove her over to the campus.

"Thank you so much, Harry. I love you for what you do for me." She started getting out of the car, stopped, turned back to me and said, "I love you. I'm glad we're friends." She kissed me and got out of the car.

I watched her disappear into the building and then drove home. Tina wasn't up yet. I made a pot of tea and since my stomach was full because of the four scones I held off on making breakfast because Tina doesn't eat much in the morning.

At nine, she and her iPad joined me and my newspaper in the dining room. I poured her a cup of tea. She nodded her thanks. Then the phone rang. She furrowed her brow and wrinkled her nose.

"Don't worry. I'll get it and I won't make you talk," I told her, then picked up the phone and said, "Wright Investigations."

"This is Ralph Lowell."

"Good morning, Mr. Lowell."

"It isn't, but—"

"Oh, I wasn't stating a fact. I was making a wish."

"Huh?"

"I was wishing you a good morning."

"Oh, I see. Well, that I could use. I'm calling to let you know, well, to ask, if you would continue working on the case."

"I see. That isn't up to me to decide, Mr. Lowell. But I'll pass your request on to Miss Wright and she'll call you later today."

"All right. I'll wait for her call. Goodbye." And I was left with a dial tone in my ear. I hung up the phone and said to Tina, "Score one for Mrs. Lowell. Mister is asking you to continue working on the case. You can call him later with your answer."

She nodded, drank tea, and continued reading her iPad.

I was feeling pretty doggone good. "Say, Boss, should I call Ed and Stinky?"

Again she nodded. Which action told me she would resume the case.

Off to the office, and when I got there, I called Ed asking him if he was available. He said he was. I told him what we wanted and that he'd be working with Stinky if he was available. Ed was good with it as long as the money was green.

I called Stinky next. He'd just finished a job and would get right on ours. I told him to call Ed Hafner and work out the details with him. He said he would and rang off.

Tina joined me in the office a little after ten. "Harry, I want David to tail Lonnie Johnson and Gwen to tail Marguerita. I want you to find out everything you can about her. Now get Lowell for me."

I punched buttons and a phone five hundred and seventy-four miles away rang. And rang five times before a voice answered.

"Mr. Lowell?"

"Yes, this is Lowell."

"Harry Wright here. Hold on. My sister wishes to speak to you."

Tina picked up her phone and motioned for me to stay on the line.

"Good morning, Mr. Lowell."

"Is yours a wish too?"

"Very much so."

"Well, Vera and I talked and decided we'd like you to continue trying to find our son."

"I will do so. But we need to talk."

"Yes, we do."

"Is now a good time?"

"It is. Well, I can make it a good time."

"Very good. Do you know how to video chat?"

"I'm not good at it, but my secretary will set it up."

"Do you use Google?"

"Yes."

"Okay. I'll be waiting for your call."

The call came through and Tina answered it. I positioned myself so I could see Lowell, but he couldn't see me.

"What I want to know," Lowell began, "is why you were spending my money to investigate Osgood and me."

"I had to eliminate Mr. Osgood as a suspect. Which I have."

"And me? I'm a suspect?"

"Mr. Lowell, I'll be frank. Something occurred between you

and your son — something out of the ordinary — which, in his mind, made leaving necessary. What was it?"

Lowell was not at all comfortable. He was fidgeting and looked as though he was even sweating.

"Your choice is simple," Tina said. "You tell me or I find out."

"This won't get back to Vera?"

"I'll keep it between us unless it turns out she needs to know."

"She won't need to know. For some years now, my secretary and I have been having an affair. Edmund found out about it. We had a big fight, and that's when he decided he was done with me and the company. He always was a momma's boy."

"I suspected as much," Tina said in reply. Whether she did or not, her saying so certainly gave her an air of omniscience. "Thank you, Mr. Lowell. One last question."

"Go ahead."

"You've had no contact of any kind with your son since he left?"

"None." He paused and cleared his throat. "Miss Wright, Vera thinks I'm cold-hearted and don't care about Edmund. But it's not true. I do care. I care very much. He's my son, after all."

"I understand, Mr. Lowell. I'll do everything I can to find out what happened to him."

"You don't think he's alive, do you?"

Tina paused, then said, "I don't know. And I don't want to give you false hope, but there is a good chance we aren't going to find him."

Lowell was quiet and still. Finally he said, "I think I understand what you're saying. Thank you, Miss Wright. Please keep us posted."

"I will, Mr. Lowell. Goodbye."

The screen went blank.

"That is one beaten man," I said.

"Yes, indeed. A difficult revelation. The knowledge your action may have resulted in the death of your hopes and dreams."

"Then again, tying your shoelaces in the morning may have the same result."

"It may."

I called David and set him on Lonnie Johnson. "And don't worry about being seen," I said, "just follow him."

"Okay. I don't get it, but Tina's the boss."

"Johnson and his roommate know we're watching so there's no use hiding."

"I see. He could try a stalking charge."

"Minnesota Statute 609.749, subdivision 7. We have a valid license to conduct surveillance and have a valid contract."

"Okay. I'll get started right away." He disconnected.

Next, I called Gwen. "Your job is to tail Marguerita Delgado Espinoza. She doesn't know you. Keep unobserved if you can. If not, don't worry about it."

"Really? What's up with that?"

"Tina was found out by Johnson using a reverse image search."

"Oh. I get it."

"Yeah. So just watch her and note what she does."

"Will do. I'll keep out of sight as long as I can."

"Thanks Gwen. Good luck." We ended the call.

Now I would see if I could find anything on Ms. Delgado Espinoza. Tina had already tried and not gotten anywhere. That didn't give me much hope. But a different brain and fresh eyes and a new day and who knows?

I started with the Toltec Land Company. Being a legal

entity, whereas Ms. Delgado Espinoza possibly being an illegal entity, I thought I might have a better shot at getting info.

At twelve-thirty Tina and I took a lunch break, after which I returned to my search. By four, I had a sizable amount of information.

The Toltec Land Company is actually owned by Toltec Enterprises, M. Maria Delgado being CEO, which is a Texas corporation formed in 2000. The address for Toltec Enterprises was a post office box in Dallas. M. Maria Delgado's address was the house on Girard in Minneapolis. Like Toltec Land Company, Toltec Enterprises was invisible. No web presence. No phone number. Nada. Zip. Zilch. Nothing.

The Toltec Land Company was started in '09. I sat back and thought about that. Logan had said Lonnie was caving three summers ago. Depending on how he was counting, three summers would be '09 or '10. A Benjamin says that's about the time he started collecting homeless men. I conveyed the info to Tina.

She nodded and smiled. I took that to mean the information was good. Very, very good.

I started searching under various combinations of Marguerita's name. The most common occurrence I found in Texas was Marguerita G. Espinoza. I found a Minnesota hit on Marguerita G. Delgado Espinoza. Clearly she was working her multiple names to her advantage.

One other name showed up in connection with Toltec Land Company. Simon Goldbaum, Esq. Attorney-at-law. In effect, he was the public face of Toltec. Although I thought his representing the company to be odd. His website advertised he was an immigration and Social Security disability lawyer.

I mentioned Goldbaum to Tina, and she said, "Why no women?"

"Come again?"

"Only homeless men. Why no women?"

"He doesn't like women?"

"Or Marguerita picks up the women."

"Could be."

"Ask Ed and Stinky to check out the women's shelters."

I called both and told them to find out if someone was offering work to homeless women. And if so, who and how many over the past three years.

"How about I pick up something from the Common Roots Café for supper?"

Tina thought for a moment and said she was okay with that. I called and ordered two lettuce wraps, two warm pretzels, two lentil tarts, and two leek and ricotta ravioli.

When I got off the phone she said, "Any meat in what you ordered?"

"No. Why?"

"Sure hope you get off this vegetarian kick real soon."

"What's the matter with vegetables?"

"Nothing. I just like meat once in a while."

"It's better if you don't kill and eat things that breathe and have brains and blood."

"So it's okay to kill and eat mushrooms, lettuce, and beans because they don't have the three Bs."

"It'd be best if we didn't kill anything. Unfortunately, the living must feast on the dead."

"Spare me the sermon and just go get our cow food."

"Such a conformist."

"Me? Hardly that, buddy. I smoke and drink madeira."

"True. Okay. Such a cannibal." And I left before I heard what she had to say in response.

Common Roots isn't far from where we live and the food is righteous. They do sell meat dishes, but I've never eaten one. Tina's had their grass-fed beef steak and their free-range chicken. She thought both were excellent. The food was ready when I got there. I paid for it and hauled it home.

I opened a bottle of Alexis Bailly Country White to drink with our meal. We ate, talked about nothing in particular, and when we were done, I put the leftovers away. Then it was back to the office to see what I could find on Goldbaum. Turns out he was almost as elusive as our subjects. He was fairly active up until 2010, and then he just kind of fell off the radar. I relayed the information to Tina, who was sitting by the fire.

"He's probably getting money from Marguerita. An interesting question is where is she getting her money."

"I've found nothing. My guess is it's all under the table."

"Probably illegal."

"Probably. Which is why I can't find anything. Although there is the apartment building and the commercial property."

"Goldbaum is probably managing those for her and that's where he's getting his money."

"Makes sense. She might be getting some, too."

"She might."

"Not sure I can do anymore damage here."

"Call it a day, Harry. We'll see what the gang comes up with."

"Sounds good." I shut the computer off and went to the kitchen to make tea. When the tea was made, I went to the library and selected the novel *The Remains of the Day*. I got comfy in my chair and turned to the first page.

14

CAMEL MEAT AND BROTHER LEONARD

FRIDAY, OCTOBER 19TH

NEITHER DAVID nor Gwen had anything earth shattering to report from yesterday other than both of our subjects were gone when they arrived, both came home about five-thirty, and both left the house in the Toyota at eight. David and Gwen followed. David got caught at a light, but Gwen made it through and kept them in sight, talking to David by phone. He caught up with the party when Johnson's Toyota had to stop for a light. David and Gwen followed them through Northeast Minneapolis. The situation becoming obvious that Johnson was trying to ditch them.

David and Gwen hung on like fleas on a hound dog. Johnson finally pulled over to the curb and stopped his car. David pulled over about seventy-five feet behind him, and Gwen pulled over about a hundred feet ahead of him. And there they all sat. For twenty minutes. Then Johnson got out of the car, walked back to David's car, and stood by the driver's door. David rolled down the window.

"May I help you?" he asked Johnson.

"Yeah, I want to know what the fuck you're doing?"

"Sitting here," David said.

"I see. A smart ass." He pulled his coat aside so David could catch a glimpse of his handgun.

David said, "Have a concealed carry permit?"

"I do, Mr. Smart Ass. So I'm asking you again, what the hell are you following me for?"

"I'm thinking I have nothing better to do on this fine October evening."

Johnson took out his cell and snapped a picture of the license plate. "Now, I'm getting a restraining order."

"Sorry, I'm a private investigator and I'm investigating. It's not going to happen for you."

"Huh. You're with that bitch, Justinia Wright."

David didn't say anything.

"Well you tell Ms. Wright if she doesn't want to have any accidents happen to her or her people, she'd best leave me and my girlfriend alone. Got it?"

David said, "You're talking to the wrong person. If you have an issue with Miss Wright, maybe you should take it up with her."

"Good. Maybe I will." Johnson walked back to his vehicle, got in, and drove off.

Of course, David and Gwen followed. But Johnson didn't go anywhere exciting. He returned home.

They phoned in early this morning, when they arrived at the Johnson-Delgado Espinoza home, and told me of yesterday's walk in the park.

After breakfast, Ed and Stinky arrived to report what they'd found. Ed spoke first, "Near as anyone can remember, Brother Leonard appeared in the spring of 2009. Stinky and I are making a guess here—"

Stinky cut in and said, "We're making an educated guess based on what people have said."

"Yeah," Ed said. "An educated guess. We figure in '09,

mebbe seven to eleven went off with him. In '10, twelve to fifteen. Last year, at least a dozen. So far this year, eleven."

Stinky said, "That's just men. A woman known as Angel Guadalupe, matching the description of Marguerita, has made the rounds of the women's shelters. In 2009, near as we could find, four women went with her. Two years ago, upwards of eight single women, two families, and four or five women with children. Last year, anywhere from six to nine women and perhaps five children. This year, four women."

Tina said, "That seems to be an awfully high number of people. If I'm following you, we're talking something over seventy-five."

"That's correct," Stinky said.

"And they have not been heard from again?" Tina asked.

"As far as anyone knows," Stinky replied.

"Over seventy-five people in three years." Tina shook her head. "This is utterly amazing."

"They're homeless," Stinky said. He shrugged. "They have no family, or haven't been in touch with their families for years. They might be mentally ill or lost their job in the recession and are now the chronically unemployed and have lost everything. Or perhaps they're immigrants, legal or illegal, and came here with nothing. They could be substance abusers. At the end of the day, they're all people no one cares about."

"Stinky's right, Miss Wright," Ed said. "They are the butt-end of society and even the government, with all its programs, doesn't really care. So when someone like Brother Leonard or this Angel Guadalupe comes along, people listen because they are desperate."

Stinky nodded in agreement.

"The magnitude is what is surprising," Tina said.

"It's big and the recession only made the plight of this class worse," Stinky said. "And very few want to truly solve the problem. Even Jesus said, 'The poor you'll always have with you.' I wish he hadn't said that."

Tina said, "I'd like you two to join David and Gwen in tailing our subjects. Coordinate your efforts with them. I have a feeling Brother Leonard and Angel Guadalupe are helping only themselves."

"We're on it, Miss Wright," Ed said.

"Thank you for the work, Miss Wright," Stinky added.

"You're welcome," she replied.

They left. I found myself shaking my head over the number of people who'd disappeared and as far as we knew, only one intrepid soul cared. Mrs. Ralph Lowell. Vera.

Tina picked up the phone. After a minute she said, "Hey, Sweet Cheeks, is it possible for you to check if you have any missing person reports gathering dust? I'm specifically looking for people reported missing who were homeless." She was quiet for a moment and then kissed the phone and said, "Bye!" She noticed me looking at her. "What?"

"You know you love him. Wouldn't it be easier if you at least lived together?"

"Things are just fine between Cal and I. Our arrangement works."

I shrugged my shoulders. "Okay. If you say so."

"Sergeant Simmons will go through the missing person reports and look for anyone who might match one of the people we're interested in."

"If so, this might turn out to be much bigger than first suspected."

"It might. And if that's the case, the government boys and girls might start to get involved."

"And there goes our fee."

"Not entirely, but they will certainly take over and sideline us."

"The trials and tribulations of being a private gumshoe."

"Indeed."

————

After lunch, I took a trip downtown and stopped by Goldbaum's office. He wasn't in, and neither was a receptionist. I tried the door. Locked. A small sign slightly above the middle of the door informed those looking at it that the office hours were Monday through Wednesday from ten to two.

"Must not need any clients," I muttered.

There was a phone number on the sign and I called it. After two rings, the voicemail came on. I got the same message I was looking at on the door, with the additional option to leave a message.

To refresh my memory, I checked the website. Same hours. There was a contact form folks could fill out. Clearly this legal beagle was not in need of money. At least from clients. He might be a first. Unless of course he was a lawyer cum politician, in which case his face would be in the public trough.

While I was out and about, I swung by the house on Nicollet Island. All quiet on the northern front. I parked and got out of my car, walked to the door, and rang the doorbell. No answer. I rang again and then a third time. An older woman answered, speaking Spanish. Other than "Si," "Buenos Dias," "Buenos Notches," "Tamale," "Taco," and "Mañana," my Spanish is non existent. I tried speaking to her in English, but she shook her head and said, "No comprehende. No English." I tipped my hat, said, "Buenos Dias," and left.

Nothing seemed out of place at the house. At least from the minuscule amount I could see into the place. Nothing seemed untoward around the house, but then only the tiny front yard was visible. I wondered if a night time expedition would yield anything? I drove on to the commercial property. The address led me to a building on East Lake. Arabic signs and writing were prominent, and Somalis thronged the place. I parked the car, got out, and paid a visit.

The enormous building seemed to house an indoor bazaar, bringing the comforts of home to Minneapolis's burgeoning Somali population. In one corner, a meat market sold halal lamb, goat, beef, chicken, and camel. On a whim, I bought a leg of goat and two pounds of cubed camel for stew. Nothing else caught my eye, although there was plenty of merchandise in dozens and dozens of booths. Prayer mats, books, clothing, prayer hats, scarves, incense, perfume, jewelry, and shoes I left, got into my car, and drove home.

I told Tina what I'd found out and announced camel stew was on the menu. She gave me a look. The kind you give a person when you wonder about their sanity. In reply, I said, "Probably tastes like chicken." She replied again with that look.

"I'll be in the kitchen preparing the stew if you need me."

She nodded, and I left.

In the kitchen, I put the meat in a bowl and poured red wine over it. I added crushed allspice, salt, pepper, and mustard powder and let it sit for an hour. I then cut up veggies for the stew and prepared vegetable stock. When the timer rang, I took the meat out of the marinade bowl and put it and the stock in the Dutch oven so it could simmer for a couple of hours, before adding the vegetables and Verdelho madeira. I tasted and adjusted the seasoning. The stew simmered for another forty-five minutes and we were ready to eat.

The phone rang. Gwen. "Hey, Harry."

"Hi, Gwen. What's up?"

"DE and LJ tried to throw us off. LJ left in his Toyota and David, Ed, and Stinky followed. I waited to make sure it wasn't a ruse. Because it sure looked like there were two people in the Toyota. Fifteen minutes after the Toyota left, the BMW pulls out. I called Stinky to let him know I needed him. He put me on hold, called David to apprise him of the situation, and then got back to me so he could pick up the tail.

"DE hit the freeway and tried to lose me there, but I stuck like glue and then Stinky joined me. She drove into St. Paul and drove around a couple of blocks and down an alley, trying to lose us. But one of us managed to hang on and then direct the other one to catch up. She then hit the freeway and got lucky. Stinky and I got separated in the traffic and she took an exit. Stinky followed but was too late. She'd vanished.

"Good work. You—"

"I'm not done."

"Oh, okay."

"Following a hunch, I told Stinky to meet me at the Nicollet Island house. Together we snooped around. The garage windows are painted so you can't see what's inside and the doors are locked. I did a no-no. I broke a window pane and took a look. Both the BMW and the van were there."

"So Marguerita is at the Nicollet Island house and Lonnie's where?"

"In South Minneapolis," she said. "Just drove around and went back home."

"Thanks Gwen."

I conveyed the info to Tina and told her supper was ready. She joined me in the dining room.

"They're probably pretty pissed off about now," Tina said.

"I suppose they are."

She started talking about Bantock and why Hollywood missed out not hiring him to compose film music.

Halfway through the monologue and stew she said, "This is actually good. You can tell the flavor isn't quite like beef, but if I didn't know any better, I might miss completely that it wasn't beef."

The monologue continued with her lamenting America's neglect of its own nineteenth-century musical heritage.

When supper was over, Tina said she'd be in the office. I cleaned up the kitchen and joined her. I found her on the loveseat in front of the fire. I sat next to her. She had a cigar going and a half-full glass of madeira on the table next to her.

"I can't shake the feeling, Harry, these two are up to something no good. Seventy-five people in three years."

The phone rang. "What's up, David?"

"Looks like Johnson is heading your way. Just letting you know you might have a visitor."

"Thanks."

I told Tina.

Her only comment was, "Interesting."

Ten minutes later, the doorbell rang. I answered the door and there on the front step was Lonnie Johnson.

"Good evening, Mr. Johnson. What may I do for you?"

He pointed out to David's and Ed's cars. "I want to talk to you about them."

I invited him in and showed him to the office. Tina was sitting at her desk. I guided him to the oversized oxblood wingback. He sat. The chair made him look a bit on the small side.

"Nice place you have here," he said.

"Thank you," Tina replied.

"What do you want?" he asked.

"The truth."

"You don't believe me?"

"No."

"That's a fine how do you do for someone trying to help our homeless problem."

"Except I don't think you are."

"What am I doing then, Ms. Wright?"

She winced.

"What's the matter?" he asked.

"It's Miss Wright," I said.

He shrugged. "Okay. Sorry. So what do you think I'm doing?"

"I can't say. But not what you pretend you're doing. Over seventy-five men, women, and children in three years. Where did they go Mr. Johnson?"

"Out west to become gainfully employed."

"That's your story and you're sticking to it."

He nodded.

"Care to share the names of the companies that employed those homeless people?"

"If I do, will that get you off my back?"

"Depends what I find out when I contact them."

"I see. You actually feel satisfied badgering people?"

"It's an honest living."

"Funny, Miss Wright. Very funny."

"Wasn't meant to be."

"So if I give you the names of companies and you can verify the people I sent there got jobs, you'll leave me alone?"

"I'm mostly interested in Edmund Lowell."

"Don't know how I can help you there. He's the one I sent home, right?"

Tina nodded.

"He must've changed his mind."

"Possible, of course. But I don't think so. Neither does his mother."

He shrugged. "You can put a fork in someone's hand, but you can't make him eat."

The two of them looked at each other for a minute. Finally he said, "I'll get you a list."

Tina said thank you, and Johnson left.

"The list will be bogus, of course," she said when I returned from door duty. "But who knows?"

All around an interesting evening. Camel stew and a meet and greet with the enemy.

15

TROUBLE ON THE ISLAND

SATURDAY, OCTOBER 20TH INTO SUNDAY, OCTOBER 21ST

CAL INVITED HIMSELF TO BREAKFAST. He also made Tina break her rule about not talking in the morning, especially business outside the office.

"Sorry, Buttercup, but two shootings occurred last night on the Northside and I'm just a little bit busy. Simmons did some checking and found four reports of homeless persons missing." He looked at a sheet of paper. "Luwanda Smith and her daughter Sierra. Reported missing by her sister, who said Luwanda went to a battered women's shelter to escape her boyfriend. Luwanda and her daughter were approached by one Angel Guadalupe offering employment out of state. Luwanda refused, went back home, and wasn't heard from again. We questioned the boyfriend, but he said she packed a suitcase while he was out. He never saw her. He died a couple of days later of a heroin overdose."

Cal looked at Tina and she nodded.

I said, "Our friend Angel. What year?"

Cal looked at the paper. "Uh, 2010. The second, also from that year. An aunt reported her niece had run away from Brainerd with her boyfriend. She was seventeen. Supposedly came here to Minneapolis. We checked the shelters and found she was at Anne's Place for a few days. Boyfriend had ditched her. The girl went off with a woman and didn't return. The staffer's new, but the story circulating around the shelter is that the woman the girl went off with could've been this Angel Guadalupe from the description.

"The other two are from last year. A Somali woman reported her daughter had run away. We actually picked her up. A friend turned her in. The girl had stayed with the friend and then gone to Anne's Place. The girl managed to get away. That was the last anyone saw of her. On the last one, we got a call from a woman in Nevada. She'd found out her run away daughter was in Minneapolis. The daughter had been in a battered women's shelter and at Anne's place, and then no more reports of her."

"Thanks, Cal. Not sure if this helps or not. Interesting that they're all women, and only one with a child."

"It is. Well, I got work to do. Catch you later."

He left, and I looked at the sheets of paper containing Simmons's notes. While interesting and confirming Vera wasn't the only concerned person, I didn't see how the information would help us.

Tina finished her tea and toast, stood, said she'd be in the office, and left. I cleaned up breakfast dishes, poured myself a cup of tea, and sat on one of the barstools. The information from Cal only confirmed there were four other concerned persons and that Angel Guadalupe was involved with two of the now missing homeless. We still did not know what was happening to these people. And I still didn't see how this had any bearing on Edmund Lowell. I finished my tea. Poured myself another cup and relocated to the office.

Tina was at her desk staring off into space. I put Simmons's notes in front of her and sat at my desk.

"Interesting, but not very helpful," I said.

She nodded. "Yes. My opinion, too. And the same will be for the list we get from Johnson."

"We know Johnson and his girlfriend are in this up to their eyeballs."

"Yes."

"But we don't know what their role is, or even what 'this' is."

"Correct."

"But they are involved in these disappearances."

"Correct."

"But we don't know if their role is legitimate or illegitimate."

"That is also correct."

"We do know Lonnie Johnson is pissed off we're bugging him."

"True."

I called Gwen. "Good morning, Sunshine. Are you still on the Island?"

"Yes. Stinky and I spent the night. I physically checked and the BMW is still in the garage. No vehicles have arrived and none have left."

"Just a minute." I conveyed the information to Tina.

She said, "Go and spell them so they can freshen up and eat."

"Gwen, I'm on my way. Let you guys have a break."

"Great. See you in a bit," she said.

I grabbed my hat and coat and drove to Nicollet Island.

Gwen got to take a break first. Since we weren't pretending to be undercover, I chatted with Stinky for a while. The night had been quiet, and they had managed to take turns getting some sleep. She was back in an hour with a thermos of mugi cha, also known as barley tea. She doesn't drink coffee or tea and isn't into caffeine.

Stinky left. I chatted a bit with Gwen. She's a fine looking woman, but we've always kept our relationship professional. I don't know for a fact, but my surmise is she keeps her personal relationships casual.

Stinky was also back in an hour. He brought doughnuts for everyone, but Gwen doesn't do sugar. He apologized and offered to get her something, but she confessed to eating a tofu and oak leaf lettuce wrap with tahini and amaranth and was quite full. Stinky and I polished off the doughnuts.

I drove to the other stakeout to check on things. David and Ed were fine. All was quiet, and they'd been able to spell each other. I drove on home.

Tina hadn't moved from the office. She was smoking a cigar and nursing a glass of madeira. I'd just gotten seated at my desk when my phone chimed. A text message from Tatty asking if I'd be joining them in their spelunking adventure tonight. I texted back telling her, no. I was working. She replied with a pouting emoticon and then a heart. I texted back an "XO."

"Who was that?" Tina asked.

"Tatty. Asking if I was going spelunking tonight. I told her no."

"She likes you."

"Yes. I know."

"Do you like her?"

"I do. But I think she's too young for anything to come of it. She'll come to her senses soon enough."

"Interesting how you said that."

"Isn't it though?"

———

The day passed quietly. I spelled Gwen and Stinky a couple times, and Tina spelled David and Ed. Along about four, we got an email from Lonnie Johnson through our website. His email said:

Below are the four businesses which employ the homeless we send out west. Marguerita's cousin, Pedro Jimenez-Espinoza, is our coordinator. He is the one who makes all the final arrangements.

There was Pedro's contact information, as well as contact information for the businesses: Delgado Truck Farms, Toltec Day Labor, Texcoco Produce, and Tlacopan Trucking. I shared the email with Tina.

She laughed. "What a pile of shit this is. Marguerita's cousin? Does he take us for fools? Very well. Find out if the companies are legit and whatever you can on Pedro."

I spent the next three hours checking out the information. There did in fact appear to be a real person by the name of Pedro Jimenez-Espinoza. He was the owner of Tlacopan Trucking. The companies also appeared to be legitimate. I called the companies, but no one answered. Next a call to Cousin Pedro, he not only answered, but he answered in Spanish. I said, "No hablo español." He said, "No hablo ingles." And there we were.

When I told Tina the results of my research, she laughed. "Let's get something to eat."

We got in her yellow Crossfire Roadster and went to Popeye's for chicken. We sat in the car and ate.

"Harry, find someone who speaks Spanish and call Cousin Pedro back. We won't get anything, but it won't be for lack of trying."

"Will do."

My phone rang, and I answered it. "Harry? Ed."

"Hey, Ed."

"Johnson just left and David and I are following."

"Okay. Keep me posted."

"Will do. Out."

I told Tina that Johnson was on the move.

She grunted an affirmation, seeing her mouth was full of chicken.

I spooned jambalaya to my mouth.

"Wonder what he's up to?" she asked.

I shrugged due to the aforesaid jambalaya.

In due course, we polished off our chicken, potatoes and gravy, biscuits, jambalaya, and coleslaw. Mighty fine eating for fast food.

"We have ice cream at home?" she asked.

I told her we did.

She started the car, put it in gear, and drove us home. Whereupon, soon after our arrival, she was spooning ice cream, cherry and chocolate chip vanilla, to her mouth. I settled for tea and Russian tea cakes.

The phone rang, and I answered.

"Hi, Harry. Ed. He led us on a merry chase. But at least one of us managed to stick to him. We followed him to Nicollet Island. We're all here. Care to join us?"

"Maybe I will. I'll check with the boss and call you back."

To Tina I said, "They're all on the Island. Want to join them?"

"No. We'll stay put. Have them keep us posted."

I called Ed back and relayed Tina's message.

To pass the time, Tina and I played backgammon. At midnight, after our tenth game, she winning ten of them, she hit the hay.

I poured myself a glass of port, sat by the dying embers in the living room fireplace, and watched their undulating glow. Somewhere in the watching, I must've fallen asleep because the next thing I was aware of was the ringing of the phone.

"Hello?" I said and checked my watch. Three a.m.

"Oh, Harry, thank God you are there. It was awful. Oh, God. They are dead and we saw it and they found us and we ran and ran."

"Tatty. Slowdown. Where are you?"

"The Island. Just Cynice and I. We don't know where Logan is. Harry, please come."

"I'm on my way." I gave her the address of the stakeout and told her to meet me there. Other detectives were there and she and Cynice would be safe with them. I woke Tina, told her there was trouble on Nicollet Island, and I was going. She told me a groggy okay, and I was off and running.

They were all together, half a block down from the house. Tatty and Cynice were half hysterical from fear, and trying to get a coherent story from them was impossible. We decided Gwen and Stinky would keep a lookout for Logan, and I would take the women to Tina's place and try to find out what happened. From the snippets we were able to get, it sounded like something out of an old pulp adventure magazine. An underground cavern, torch light, an altar, and human sacrifice.

16

SACRIFICE
SUNDAY, OCTOBER 21ST

CYNICE, Tatty, and I were back home by four. I woke Tina.

The young ladies were very much shaken by what they'd seen and Logan's disappearance. I made hot chocolate for my friends. The odor of weed was definitely present on their hair and clothes. We got them settled enough for the two to tell us what happened.

"We were at my apartment," Cynice began. "I got a fresh bag of weed and we rolled several joints and smoked them before going to the Island. Everything was like usual, except Logan took a tunnel we hadn't taken before. It seemed older than the other tunnels. The brick was more crumbly. We found a side tunnel that was sealed off."

"About thirty feet in," Tatty said, "and it had a decline of, I'd say, five degrees."

"Yeah," Cynice concurred, "but there was a crack in the bricks and Logan thought we could make it bigger and squeeze through."

"I'd brought a chisel-tip rock hammer along, just in case," Tatty said, "and we used that to break up the brick. The hammer was light-weight, but the brick was, um, like rotten wood and broke up easily."

"So Logan made an opening for us to go through," Cynice continued. "The air was stale and damp."

"Damp?" I said.

"Yes," Tatty said. "My guess is the tunnel goes under the river."

Cynice went on, "We walked, what, ten feet?"

Tatty nodded.

"Ten feet and steps appeared. We took the steps down. The sides and roof of the tunnel were wet and no longer brick but stone."

"Solid stone," Tatty added.

"Yeah. Solid stone and kind of slimy. I counted the steps. Fifty-seven. The tunnel wasn't long, and it entered a room."

"'One of the lost caves of Nicollet Island,' Logan announced to us," Tatty said.

"And it was a big mother, too," Cynice added.

"I think it is under the river," Tatty said. She continued, "It was a natural cave. There was a hole in the middle of the floor. Logan dropped a pebble and figured the drop was about fifty feet. There were several chambers connected to the main chamber. It was quite beautiful. Flowstone, stalagmites and stalactites, some drapery, and soda straws. At the far end was an opening with a descending slope of I'd guess one foot for every three."

"I didn't want to go any further," Cynice said, "but Logan insisted. I was scared."

"I was uneasy about it, too," Tatty said. "We hadn't marked our path, and I was nervous. I told Logan I'd have to go back and make some marks. He was angry, but told me to go ahead. I went back making marks in the floor with my hammer until I got to the stairs. Then I returned to where Logan and Cynice were waiting and we continued our descent. Every ten feet, I made a mark, so we'd find our way back."

"God, Tatty, I'm so glad you did," Cynice said.

Tatty continued, "The passage became very narrow, and we had to squeeze through. Then it opened into a small room. The stone was wet and our clothes were very wet by the time we got to the room."

"What do you mean?" Cynice said. "We were soaked."

"Yes, we were," Tatty conceded.

"And then we were in that small room," Cynice said. "And we could hear drumming from somewhere. Logan found a crack in the wall. Not very wide but wide enough to see through and that's when we realized there was light coming from the other side."

"Light?" Tina said.

"Yes," Tatty affirmed.

"What kind of light?" I asked.

"Electric light," Cynice said, "and lots of it. There were a whole bunch of people in the room beyond."

"How many? Any idea?" I asked.

Cynice thought a moment. "I don't know. Lots."

"And they were all facing one direction," Tatty said.

"Towards the brightest lit area," Cynice added.

"It was like we were kind of to the side and back," Tatty explained, "and there was a raised platform and a kind of short pillar on the platform. There was also a hut behind the pillar."

"And this woman was standing with her arms in the air, kinda like doing rap in a foreign language," Cynice said.

"It was a chant," Tatty clarified.

"Whatever," Cynice said. "And when she was done, they brought out a man. Naked. And laid him on the pillar — Oh, God—" Cynice shook her head.

I finished for her, "And the woman took a knife, cut out his heart, and then carried it back to the hut."

They both nodded and Cynice had the dry heaves.

"Good God," Tina said.

Tatty took a deep breath and continued. "Cynice started to scream, but I got my hand over her mouth."

Tears were running down Cynice's cheeks. "But they heard it. That's when we found out there was an opening from where we were to the larger chamber."

"Not a large opening, but large enough," Tatty said.

Cynice took over, "Three or four men were suddenly with us and Logan was wrestling with one and Tatty hit another with her hammer. One tried grabbing me and I kicked him. Logan told us to run and Tatty got a good hit on the one Logan was wrestling with and Logan punched him and he fell."

"Logan took the hammer from me," Tatty said, "and told me to 'run like hell'. Cynice and I got through the narrow passage, but we had the incline to climb and it was wet. I looked back and Logan made it through the narrow passage. I heard a yell and a sickening thunk and feet running behind me. Logan's voice kept saying, 'run, run'. We got up the slope and Cynice and I bolted across the chamber following the marks I'd made. I looked back and saw Logan hurl a rock down the passageway. I stopped. He saw me and yelled, 'run'. He threw another rock, and I ran after Cynice."

Cynice, choking back sobs, got out, "He didn't make it."

"This is important," Tina said. "Can you go back?"

Cynice's eyes were big and round and Tatty was shaking. I moved so I could put my arms around them.

Cynice's voice was a whisper, "Do we have to?"

"If you want to find Logan you do," Tina said.

"I'm, I'm not sure how to get to that sealed passage we opened," Tatty said. "Logan was leading."

"Can you try?" Tina pressed.

Tatty took a deep breath reached out and took Cynice's hand. They looked at each other and nodded.

Tina was on the phone. "Sweet Cheeks we have two young women who may have just witnessed a murder. Where? You won't believe it. Beneath Nicollet Island."

————

I checked my watch. The time was three minutes after six. There were seven of us in the tunnel. Cal and Sergeant Simmons, two flat feet by the names of Thompson and Thomson, Tatty and Cynice, and myself. Tatty was in the lead followed by yours truly, then Cal, then Cynice, and finally Simmons, Thompson, and Thomson.

After a good twenty minutes, Tatty found the old tunnel that looked to be the one Logan had taken, but there was no side tunnel. After twenty steps, Tatty said we needed to go back. We'd gone too far.

Swenson said, "Listen up. We're going back. Keep your eyes and sense of touch sharp. We might have missed what we're looking for."

Back we went, carefully checking the wall inch by inch. Simmons spotted it. "Lieutenant. I think this section here looks new." Tatty made her way to where Simmons was standing. "Yes. This is new," she confirmed. I looked at it. It was one of those prefab sheets of brick that had been quickly and somewhat hastily cemented into place. Cal joined me.

"Well, Major," he said, "looks as though someone doesn't want anyone going down this corridor."

"That's what it looks like to me," I replied.

"We're going to have to get a sledge to break through," Cal added. "You don't happen to have one, do you?"

"No."

"All right," Cal said. "We're going back up."

We were all top side by five after seven. Another three hours before the hardware stores opened. I said that to Cal.

He laughed and put his arm around me. "Harry, my man, we do-it-yourselfers go to the big box stores. They're open now."

Needless to say you can guess I'm not a do-it-yourselfer.

Cal dispatched Thomson and Thompson to get a couple of sledge hammers and goggles pronto. I asked Tatty and Cynice if they were up to getting breakfast for all of us. Tatty didn't have a valid driver's license and Cynice said she didn't think so. I went instead. On my way, I phoned home and told the boss lady what we'd found out and what we were going to do about it.

I went to White Castle and ordered a dozen breakfast toasted egg and cheese sandwiches, a dozen Hash Brown Nibblers, and three dozen Breakfast Sliders with bacon, egg, and cheese. I hauled the food back and parceled the grub out to the boys and girl on the stakeout. Gwen frowned but took a Nibbler and a sandwich. The remainder I hauled back to Spelunkers Anonymous. Thompson and Thomson pulled up when I did. They hadn't been able to agree and ended up with seven different sledges. Even I could tell a couple of them weren't at all suited for the job.

We wolfed down the sandwiches, sliders, and hash browns and went back to the tunnels. Second time around the spot was easy to find. Swenson ordered the flat feet to have at it. Like working on a chain gang they eventually got into the swing of things and the wall came a tumblin' down. In we went. But where Logan had used Tatty's hammer earlier to break open the old seal on the passage, there was fresh cement and mortar.

Swenson was pissed. "Goddamn it. Someone sure as hell wants to make sure this passage remains sealed. Thompson, Thomson, go get those sledges. You get a repeat performance."

And after a solid ten to fifteen minutes of sledgehammer blows, the second wall came a tumblin' down. The air was damp, and I thought it smelled musty and moldy, like an old damp basement.

"The steps are up ahead," Tatty said.

I called back, "Steps up ahead. Be careful, it's a long way to the bottom."

We descended the stairs and entered the cave. We directed our flashlight beams around the large chamber I couldn't resist, I took out my cell and snapped pictures.

"It's very beautiful, is it not?" Tatty said.

"Very," I replied.

The stalagmites and stalactites in places had met and formed columns. The drapery was amazing. The rock looked exactly like drapes. I can't remember seeing flowstone and soda straws. They were simply fascinating.

"Look down," Tatty said. "There is a deep hole up ahead."

We found the hole, and we found Logan.

"Oh my God, oh my God," Cynice said. "Logan, Logan are you alive?"

He didn't answer, and she started screaming.

To Simmons, Cal said, "Take her up and call for help. We have to get him out of there."

Cynice didn't want to go but Tatty talked to her and the two of them went with Simmons.

Cal, the flat feet, and I played our flashlights into the hole. It was indeed a good fifty feet down. If Logan was alive, he was probably pretty badly busted up.

I called down, "Logan, buddy, Cynice is waiting for you. Are you alive?"

Then miracle of miracles he moved his arm.

"Holy shit," Thomson, or perhaps it was Thompson, said.

"Hang in there, Logan," I yelled. "We're getting help. Hang in there for Cynice."

Of course in situations like that everything seems to take forever. Everything moves in slow motion. And nothing goes according to plan. Cal sent Thompson topside to find out what was taking so long. Thompson met Simmons escorting the rescue team when he was halfway back to the surface and relieved Simmons, bringing the team the rest of the way. They got Logan out and almost lost him when one of the stretcher bearers slipped on the steps. Getting him up through the manhole took forever, but they finally managed it and by noon Logan was on his way to the hospital. Cal sent Simmons, with Tatty and Cynice, to the hospital to see if he could get a statement.

Then to me, he said, "Well, Harry, you up for going back down there and see if we can make anything out of this story?"

"Let's do it," I replied.

Once again Cal, the flat feet, and I descended into the netherworld below Nicollet Island. We searched that big, beautiful subterranean chamber, and one of the flat feet found Tatty's hammer marks on the floor; which we followed. That brought us to the decline and it wasn't long before we reached the fat man's agony. My flashlight also picked up Tatty's hammer. There was blood on it. Cal slipped it into an evidence bag.

We played our flashlights on the fissure. There was no way Cal was going to get through there. Thompson confessed his claustrophobia was at its limit. Thomson tried but too many beers gave him a bulge he just couldn't suck in long enough to make it. That left me. I'm about average build, but a bit bulkier than Logan. Bulk happens in middle-age. The flashlight revealed the fissure to cut through about seven feet of rock.

"You don't have to, Harry," Cal said.

I took a deep breath and exhaled. "I'll try it." I went in sideways and had millimeters to spare. And the rock was wet. I came back out and stripped down to my underwear.

"You're going to catch your death and Tina will never forgive me," Cal said.

"Tell her I love her and I made my own stupid decision."

Back at it. I slide in sideways. God, that water was cold. But without my clothes I had more room and slid through pretty easily. I called back, "I'm through. I see blood on the floor. Not a lot." I looked through the fissure Tatty and Cynice had spoken of, but didn't see anything because it was too dark. It took a bit of playing with the flashlight, but I found the entrance to the main grotto. This was one mammoth cave. Up and down and back and forth, I played the flashlight around and guessed somewhere around a hundred could comfortably fit in the chamber.

Looking back in the direction where I entered, I turned around and guessed at where the altar must have been. But playing the flashlight in long sweeps revealed there was nothing there. I walked up to it, or where it should have been from Tatty's and Cynice's description, just to be sure, but there was nothing manmade. Just rock. The chill air was slowly turning my bones to ice. I'd left my cell behind. So no pictures. I retraced my steps, sidled through the fat man's agony, and saw three relieved faces.

"Come on, Harry, get dressed and let's get you home," Cal said.

A shower, supper, and a tale of adventure later, Cal, Tina, and I were perplexed what to do.

"We have Tatty's and Cynice's stories," Tina said, "and if Logan pulls through, we'll have his."

"But they were smoking dope and Harry saw nothing. No evidence to back up their story," Cal said.

"There is the hammer," I said.

"There is," he conceded. "But it won't prove what they claim to have seen."

"According to David, our suspected villains are holding tight in the house," Tina said.

Cal shook his head. "I need more. There's nothing to connect what they saw to Johnson, his woman, or that house."

Tina sighed. "Very well, Cal. Thanks."

"At least we got that kid out of a sure death situation," Cal said. Then added, "Goddamn sewer rats."

He got up and Tina walked him to the door. When she came back, she said, "From your description, I think David and Gwen could make it. I want the three of you to go down there with a camera and photograph the place."

"Now?"

"Yes. Now. And if you can figure out how to do it, bug the place."

"You don't want much, do you?"

"Nope. Just what I need."

17

KIDNAPPED!

FOR THE UMPTEENTH TIME, I was going back underground. I was beginning to feel like a troglodyte. This time, David and Gwen were with me. I'd explained what Tina wanted, and both were game. Ed and Stinky were above ground with a map, giving them a rough idea, very rough, of where we were going.

I was familiar enough with the route, so I had no trouble guiding us to the beautiful and large chamber containing the hole that Logan had fallen into. David and Gwen were awestruck by what they saw.

"Right here in Minneapolis," Gwen said.

"And right under our feet," David added. "I wonder who made the steps to get here and why no one ever exploited this place?"

"We'll probably never know," I said.

After some time playing tourist, and the beauty of the cave was such I didn't begrudge the time, we moved on through the far passage that led to the fat man's agony.

David simply said, "Wow."

Gwen's eyes moved from the fissure, to me, and back to the

fissure. She pointed at the narrow gap in the rock. "You made it through there?"

"Geez, Gwen, you make it sound like I'm the circus fat man or something."

"Sorry, Harry, it's just, well, it's pretty narrow. Kinda gives me the willies."

"You don't have to go through," I replied.

"Let me think about it," she said.

"Sure," I replied.

David studied the fissure, looked me up and down, and said, "If you can do it, I can do it."

"Have at it," I said.

He turned sideways and sidled through.

"Why don't you stay here," I said to Gwen. "Be good if we had someone on the other side. Just in case."

"Sure. Thanks, Harry."

I stripped down to my undies, grabbed my bag of spelunking essentials, and sidled through the gap. Once through, I pulled out a towel, dried off, and put on the light trousers and shirt I'd carried with me.

David said, "You were a Boy Scout."

"It shows, eh?"

He smiled and nodded.

He followed me into the main chamber. After shining his light around, he said, with reverence in his voice, "Awesome."

We set up the small but bright lights and took our pictures. After discussing with David, I gave up on the idea of bugging the place. No matter how many possibilities we considered, we were pretty sure we wouldn't get a signal out and had no guarantee we could retrieve a recording.

Each of us took one last look around the grotto and then made our way to the little room and sidled through the fissure. But when we got to the other side, there was no Gwen. No signs of a struggle. Nothing seemed to be missing except for Gwen.

"This just hit home," David said.

"Yeah."

"Do you think her willies got the best of her and she decamped?"

"Let's hope."

"I don't like the sound of that, Harry."

"I don't either, David."

"Could they have snatched her?"

"It's possible."

David let out a whistle. "And it's looking very probable."

"Let's get going. Pray we find her on the way back."

We retraced our steps, but no dice. We shined our lights in the hole, but it was empty. We called her name and got silence in response. I was disheartened and mad as hell all at the same time. When the fresh air of the upper world caressed my face, I phoned Tina and told her what happened. The one word expletive that came as a reply I took to mean she wasn't a happy camper.

"Instructions?" I queried of the silence on the other end.

"I want everyone here. Now."

Yup. Not a happy camper.

———

Tina was at her desk and she definitely wasn't happy. The scowl on her face and the furrows in her forehead and above her nose and around her lips, which she displayed now, were reserved for those times when she was utterly pissed off. And I'd only seen them twice at most, now thrice, in the time I've been with her. David sat in the oversized wingback, Ed and Stinky occupied the chesterfield, and I was at my desk.

"They've gone on the offensive," Tina said. "Was everyone still at the Nicollet Island house?"

"They were," Ed said.

"It's one-thirty now. David, are you willing to do some breaking and entering?"

"I am now," he said.

"I want you to break into the house on Girard and see what you can find."

"Anything in particular?"

"No. Whatever may have a bearing on finding Gwen."

"I'm off," David said and left.

"Ed, I want you to set a fire at the Nicollet Island place."

Ed swallowed.

"Just something to get some official people there."

"Okay." He stood up to leave when we heard the sound of breaking glass.

Ed and I bolted out of the office. Stinky was right behind us. Tina bringing up the rear. On the floor in the foyer was a rock with a note tied to it. I picked it up. The note was hand-written in a small, neat script. It read:

Friends are a valued possession. If you wish yours returned, stop all activity and drop your case.

I handed the note to Tina. She turned it over to check the back and then read it.

"Do we stop David?" she asked.

"Might give us ammo," I replied.

She nodded. "Ed, go make your ruckus."

"Yes, Miss Wright," he replied, and left.

"Do you know Spanish, Stinky?"

"Some. Not enough to carry on a conversation."

"Do you know anyone who does?"

"I do."

"Can you get them at this hour?"

"She'll probably be working."

"I see. Get her. Harry, give Stinky money. Get her and when the fire truck arrives, see if you can talk to people."

I got money for Stinky, and he left.

"Harry, go to the hospital and make sure the girls are okay."

"You going to be all right here, alone?"

"I was a CIA field operative." She walked backed to her desk, and I followed to the office doorway. She opened her middle desk drawer, took out her forty-five caliber pistol, and racked the slide. "I'll be fine. Now go."

18

SURRENDER

MONDAY, OCTOBER 22ND

TATTY AND CYNICE were in a lounge. The last word they'd had was Logan was pretty badly busted up, but he'd apparently landed on his feet and that saved his life. He was still in surgery as of forty-five minutes ago. Sergeant Simmons had left. But would be back later, he'd told them.

"How're you two holding up?"

Cynice nodded.

"We'll be okay, Harry," Tatty said.

I filled them in on the night's excitement after Logan had been carted off to the hospital, but not on David's, Ed's, or Stinky's missions. Some things are best left unsaid.

Cynice's voice was flat and lifeless. "They have her. They're going to kill her, aren't they? It's what they do to people, isn't it?"

"I think so." I pulled out a picture of Marguerita and showed it to them. "Is this the woman who was chanting and had the knife?"

Cynice shrugged. "There was light, but the place was still kind of dark. It could've been her."

Tatty said, "Sorry, Harry, it's what Cynice said."

"That's okay. Don't worry about it."

Tatty touched my arm. "How are you going to get your friend back?"

"I don't know."

My phone rang. Tina. I said, "Hi. Good news?"

"No. Come home as soon as you can."

"On my way."

"Trouble?" Tatty asked.

"Looks like it. Gotta go. Are you two good?"

Tatty nodded. "We'll be fine, Harry. This is a hospital."

"Okay." I hugged her and Cynice and then took off for home.

Back at the ranch, I found David, Ed, and Stinky had preceded me.

"Doesn't look good for the home team," I said.

"It isn't," Tina said. "David set off their alarm system. Ed didn't get to set the fire because the rats were abandoning ship. And the old woman at the place said — What was it, Stinky?"

"The old woman told my friend, and I quote, 'The devil has many eyes. Go away. No one here. The devil has many eyes.' Then she closed the door on us."

"Stinky was there about a half-hour after Ed," Tina said. "Then, after the guys were back, I get this." She pointed to a box. "Rang the doorbell, and this box was on the porch."

The box was full of hair, the color of dark chocolate. There was a note. I read:

This will grow back, other body parts do not. Your friend will stay whole if you stop.

.   .   .

I looked at Tina. She was visibly upset. Since working with my sister, I've gathered she has a special fondness for Gwen, who is just about her only friend.

"Should we call in Cal?" I asked.

"I suggested the same, Harry," David said.

I sat at my desk. "I'd say you didn't. Otherwise he'd be here."

"No, I didn't," Tina said. "Is there anything we can do? Or do we turn this over to the police?"

"This is Gwen, Tina," I said. "We don't have the manpower. She's like family."

She nodded. "Okay." She picked up her cell, told it to call Cal, and waited. After what was probably a couple rings, we heard her say, "Cal, Gwen's been kidnapped."

———

Flashing lights and sirens are a definite plus when you want to get somewhere quickly. I could be wrong, but I don't think five minutes passed after Tina hung up before our doorbell was ringing and the person on the step ringing it was Cal Swenson.

I let him in. He said hello, and marched into the office. I was right behind him.

"When did you last see her?" he asked.

"Around one," I said, making my way to my desk.

"This morning?"

"Yes," I replied.

"What the hell took you—?" He stopped and wheeled to face Tina. "Wait. I know. You were trying to do something fancy. Weren't you?"

Tina didn't say anything.

"Jesus H. Christ. Where did you last see her?"

I said, "Under Nicollet Island."

He turned to me. "You went back there?"

"Yes."

He just shook his head and plopped down into the oversized wingback. David had vacated it for him.

Tina spoke, "Look at this box, Cal, and the note."

He got up, and stood next to the desk. She held out the rock and note to him first, then he looked at the box. "Jesus," was all he said and sat back down. "I need these for forensics to go over." He ran his fingers through his hair. "Okay. We have a kidnapping case. But nothing to tie it to Johnson or his girlfriend unless their prints or DNA are on that stuff."

"We need to get into that house, Cal," Tina said.

"There is no reason to search that house. No judge is going to issue a search warrant unless we can establish a connection. And so far, there isn't one."

"There is," Tina said.

"None a judge would see, even with a microscope."

The silence was thick. I don't know how much time passed, maybe a couple seconds that only seemed to be centuries. Cal spoke, "I know. This is Gwen. I'll pass this on and they'll organize a search party. Right now, that's the best we can do."

"Very well." Tina's voice was resigned. But her eyes weren't.

Cal left with the rock and box. I saw him to the door and returned to my desk.

Tina spoke, "We're going to get Gwen back and then we're going to blow this cult sky high."

"What do you want us to do?" David asked.

"Right now, nothing. You three go home. But I'm asking you to be ready. Harry, I want you to deliver the surrender note I'm writing. If you use the same method of delivery they did, I won't mind."

"You're the boss," I replied. I walked our friends to the door and returned to my desk.

"Here. Make a copy." She handed me her note.

I read:

You win. Please release our friend. We shall cease and desist immediately.

I made a copy and left.

One would think rocks and scrap metal would be the easiest things to find. And they are, but not when you're looking for them. Then, it is as if they suddenly decide to hide in the trash cans where they belong in the first place.

I finally found a glass soda pop bottle that was clear. I wanted to make sure they would see the note. And I picked up what looked to be half a brick. I rubber banded the note to the brick and set out to deliver the messages.

Daylight was still very abundant, which made delivery something of a problem if I was going tit for tat and I saw no reason not to.

I parked four blocks away from the Girard house, hoofed it there, hurled the brick through their picture window, and ran like hell. I ran south, then west, up Hennepin, back east, and south again to my car. I certainly got my exercise in for the day.

Unfortunately, I had a repeat performance to make at the house on Nicollet Island.

I parked at Surdyck's, hoofed the ten blocks to the house on the island, hurled my pop bottle, and ran like hell back to the liquor store. To make the best use of the situation, I bought cheese and wine.

Messages delivered, I drove home. Tina was still in the office.

"Delivered in kind," I said. "Picked up some cheese and wine. You know. Food always makes things better."

"Thank you," Tina said.

"I just hope we haven't been hoodwinked."

"Me, too."

19

GWEN

TUESDAY MORNING, OCTOBER 23RD

THE POLICE DEPARTMENT sent two dozen men into the tunnels beneath Nicollet Island. Six hours later, two of which were spent trying to find the five of their own who'd gotten lost, they called a halt to the search, having found nothing.

Cal called us at eight this morning to let us know. Twenty minutes later, the doorbell rang at the side door. When I got there, through the window, I saw a tied up, drugged, and bald Gwen Poisson.

I grabbed a knife, rushed outside, and cut the cords. She was very groggy. After a bit of effort, I got her to sit up. Then, I put my arms around her, hoisted her into a standing position, and manhandled her into the house. I let her slide to the floor, ran upstairs, got Tina, and together we got Gwen stretched out on a sofa in the living room.

With Tina taking care of Gwen, I called Cal.

"What is it, Major?"

"Whoever took Gwen just dropped her off at our side door. Talk to you later. I'm calling an ambulance."

I dialed 911 and within minutes an ambulance was at our door and Gwen was off to the hospital, with a hastily dressed Tina and I following. On the way, I called David, Ed, and Stinky to let them know Gwen had been returned and we were heading to the hospital to have her checked out.

Other than her being drugged, Gwen looked to be in good condition according to the ER doctor. They'd keep her for a day to make sure. Tina stayed with her and I went to find Logan's room and hopefully Tatty and Cynice. He was in Intensive Care. Tatty and Cynice were in the lounge and so were a man and a woman. Given the likeness, I guessed them to be Logan's parents.

"How's Logan?" I asked.

"His feet and leg bones were pretty busted up," Cynice said. "These are Logan's parents, Bob and Cindy."

I introduced myself and shook hands with them.

Cindy said, "The doctors said he's lucky to be alive. They don't know if he'll be able to walk. His bones were shattered. But we're hopeful."

"He's a determined guy," I said. "My money says he'll give it his best shot.

"Thank you," she said.

To Cynice and Tatty I said, "Gwen's safe."

"I'm so glad, Harry," Cynice said.

"That's wonderful! Is she okay?" Tatty asked.

"The doctors think so. They're keeping her for observation. Tina's with her. Can Logan have visitors?"

"Not yet," Bob said.

"Perhaps tomorrow," Cindy added.

"I'll stop back," I said. "Nice meeting you." I shook hands with Bob and Cindy.

I walked back to Gwen's room. She was more lucid, but still not a hundred percent.

"Are we really giving this up?" I asked Tina.

"For now," Tina said. "I want to hear what Gwen has to say before I decide whether we do anything more."

"Okay. You're the boss. Do you want to say anything to the Lowells?"

"Not yet."

"I'll get us some breakfast."

"Thanks, Harry."

After a bit of searching, I found the cafeteria. Personally, I think hospital food is only beaten by army food when it comes to awarding the blue ribbon for worst food in the solar system. I opted for a couple of fruit bowls, milk, and pre-fab cereal. It's pretty difficult to mess up raisin bran made by a respected cereal manufacturer.

I took the tray back up to Gwen's room. Tina took one look and wrinkled her nose.

"Look. This is a hospital. Not a five-star restaurant. It's not even Mac and Don's. I picked the best they had to offer."

After considerable thought and much hemming and hawing, she took the cereal and milk.

"You can have one of the fruit bowls," I said.

She shook her head. "I have no clue how long that's been wrapped in plastic, sitting in that plastic bowl, and absorbing God knows what out of the plastic." She shuddered at the thought of what that fruit might have already morphed into.

"You should've been in the army. You learn to eat anything."

"No, thank you."

We ate while Gwen slept. Every now and then, she'd open her eyes, and we'd say 'hi' to her and tell her everything was going to be okay. She'd mumble something and then doze off again. When we were done eating, I took the tray down to the cafeteria. On the way back, I swung by the lounge outside ICU to find out if there was an update on Logan. Tatty and Cynice were sleeping. Bob said nothing had changed and thanked me for stopping by.

Gwen's eyes were open when I returned and she was talking a bit, but still somewhat groggy. We understood her to say she thought she'd been shot with a stun gun and then drugged. She dozed off. But the next time she woke, she was much more coherent and was able to tell us what happened.

"I was waiting for you, Harry, and David to come back when I heard a noise. I turned and saw two men. One fired the stun gun before I could yell. I couldn't do anything. They took me up the incline to the large chamber. I was beginning to regain control of my muscles when they gagged me and injected something into me. I think it might have been heroin. My God, the rush and euphoria was better than anything. Even sex. After that, I was pretty much out of it. I do remember they put me in a room with other people. I was too doped up to think of counting how many were there."

"Did they keep you doped?" Tina asked.

"Pretty much. When the effects wore off, the room was different, I think, then the first one I was in. But I can't be sure. I was with two other women. They were too doped up to give me any information. Then three men came in. Two held me down and the third injected me. Then the next thing I know, I'm here."

"You don't remember being at my place?" Tina asked.

Gwen shook her head. "And they cut my hair. Shaved my head."

Tina told her the story from our end.

"So now what?" Gwen asked.

"You rest," Tina said. "I want to make sure you're back to normal."

"Yeah, but—"

"No, buts," Tina said. "We'll get them. I just have to figure out how."

————

How indeed was the question. In my mind, the bigger question was why'd they give up Gwen? Did they actually hope to get Tina to stop? The little hunch-center in my brain was telling me no. They knew we knew there was something dark, evil, and sinister going on in that cave. I didn't think it likely they would abandon it unless they had either an alternative in place or could get us off their backs so they could return to it. Thus far, their actions suggested either.

If they had an alternative place for their hideous rituals, we were sunk. Because it could be anywhere. Our best bet lay in them returning to the cave and going on as before. And if the cave was their choice, then there had to be another entrance to it. Most likely one from the house and that's why Tina was so determined to get in there. And if there was another entrance, then it didn't matter if they bricked up the one we went through because they didn't need it.

So why return Gwen? It didn't make sense to me, unless they actually thought Tina would leave them alone. Surely they weren't that naïve? Most likely, they had something else up their sleeve. The question was, what?

20

LIGHT BULB

TUESDAY EVENING, OCTOBER 23RD

TINA GOT the hospital to release Gwen early. There was nothing wrong with her. The drugs had worn off by afternoon and she was back to her old self, sans hair. In the interest of safety, Gwen was staying with us for a few days.

Bob and Cindy had insisted Cynice and Tatty go home and get some sleep, decent food, and attend their classes. The young women finally capitulated. Cynice went to her parents's place and Tatty came home with us. There's plenty of sleeping space. Six extra bedrooms, to be exact.

Supper wasn't anything fancy. I didn't have time to cook. Instead, I picked up two take and bake pizzas and whipped up a salad. For Gwen, a vegetarian pizza. For Tina, a pepperoni pizza. Tatty and I shared both. I opened a bottle of Alexis Bailly Country Red and made cucumber-infused water for Gwen.

Our mealtime conversation revolved around sustainable agriculture and eating for the planetary survival of the greatest number of species.

"We have to stop eating our fellow creatures," Gwen said. "We are wiping out wild stocks; we are engaging in massive pollution of our groundwater due to animal waste from feed lots; and excreted hormones, drugs, and antibiotics are wreaking havoc on wild animals — both on land and in the sea."

Tina took a bite of pepperoni pizza. "What you are proposing we do is impossible."

"To stop eating meat and animal products?" Yes, Gwen was back to normal. Except for her bald head. "If we continue like this, it will be Soylent Green."

"Perhaps. But the real cause," Tina picked up a pepperoni slice that had somehow escaped from her pizza, "is that there are simply too many people on the planet."

Gwen was excited and picking up steam. "Exactly! Humans have to stop reproducing."

Tina asked, "How is our extinction going to help us? Or the planet? Nature successfully wiped out thousands of species before PETA was ever around to protest. Nature might successfully do so again and next time she might choose us."

I decided to play. "Yellowstone could blow any day now. Poof. There'd go the United States and most if not all the life on the planet from the subsequent volcanic ash, gases, and volcano-induced climate change. Would that work for you, Gwen?"

"Harry, I'm surprised at you," Gwen shot back. "You're two-thirds the way to being a vegetarian."

"True. But not at the expense of getting rid of people," I replied.

"But people are the problem."

I was reaching for a slice of veg pizza. "I'll grant you that, Gwen. But your solution of no reproduction won't help the problem."

"Why?"

Pizza slice in hand, I leaned back in my chair. "Because

only the brightest and best will follow it. The poor farmer who has to slash and burn to eke out a living and needs ten kids to help him do so isn't going to listen to you, and he's part of the problem. Perhaps the major part."

Tatty chimed in, "If I may, I think the need for more is the problem. The mindset of not being satisfied with what we have. If we could see how easy it is to be satisfied with very little, we wouldn't ruin this lovely world trying to get more."

"And don't forget profit," Gwen said.

"But the desire for money," Tatty explained, "comes from a mind saying, 'I don't have enough yet.'"

"Tatty has a point," I said. "When my wife told me to leave because I was no longer providing a paycheck, I quickly found out what was important in life. And it wasn't having a Beemer. It was being happy that today was a good day because I'd gotten three hots and a cot."

Tatty nodded in approval. "Yes. That is what I'm trying to say. What is the most important thing is to be with the people who bring you joy and doing the things that bring you happiness. And to be content with what you have."

Gwen raised her glass of cucumber infused water. "To friends who truly care if you live or die and remember you like cucumber water."

We all raised our glasses and said, "Cheers!"

"So is this done now? Your case?" Tatty asked.

Tina shook her head and the look in her eyes spoke volumes. "No, it is not done."

"But Gwen is back with us," Tatty continued.

"Yes, she is," Tina replied, "and I'm grateful beyond words, but there are other people who are not free and we know they are prisoners and that they will meet a horrible death if we don't do something soon."

"Good," Tatty said. "Because I shall not forget that awful scene. It was too horrible."

I leaned forward and, in spite of Miss Manners, or maybe to spite her, put my elbows on the table. "The question is how. We have no real evidence and I hate to say it, but we need to find a body or two or some bones."

Tina thought for a moment and while doing so picked up a slice of pizza, took a bite, chewed, and swallowed. "Harry, your earlier description was of an Aztec ritual, was it not?"

"Yes."

"So what do they do with the bodies?"

I nodded to indicate I knew where she was going with her question. "Good question. Part of Aztec worship was ritual cannibalism."

Tina continued. "Which means they'd only have bones left."

"True."

"But no bones have been found."

"True, again."

"So where are they?"

I leaned back in my chair, pursed my lips for a moment, then said, "They either have an ossuary or they dissolve them in acid or lye."

"Good God," Gwen blurted.

"It is our hope," I said.

"What?" Gwen shot back, her face showing she was puzzled.

"That God is good," I explained.

Three women rolled three pairs of eyes.

Tatty said, "Harry, you are a dear, sweet man, but sometimes you are very strange."

Tina and Gwen burst out laughing and Gwen said, "Sister, you haven't seen nothing yet."

"Gee, thanks," I protested. "The problem is clearly too much estrogen in this house."

That cracked them up even more.

"So you prefer testosterone, is that it?" Gwen said.

"Good grief." There was nothing more to be done but to ignore them, eat pizza, and drink wine, which is what I did.

———

After supper we retired to the family room. Tatty was reading some thick tome for class. Tina was smoking a cigar and listening to music through headphones. Gwen was watching a movie on her iPad. And I was reading.

The phone rang. I answered and got Cal's voice. "Hey, Major. Just letting you know, those items came out clean. Can't trace them to anyone." I told him we appreciated the follow up. I passed the info on to Tina.

"I'm not surprised," she said.

"They run a pretty sharp operation," Gwen said. "No chinks in the armor."

"Not that we've found," Tina replied.

"We may have to make a direct assault here," I said.

"What's that mean?" Gwen asked.

"It means Harry has been playing too many war games lately," Tina answered for me.

"It does not," I said.

"Well, too much chess then," Tina shot back.

Tatty spoke up, "No. He's into Halloween chess."

Tina rolled her eyes. "Whatever the hell that means."

Tatty just laughed and continued reading her book. After all it isn't really something you can explain to non-chess players.

"What I mean is," I began, "we may need to take them on

directly. If you want to get into that house, then maybe you need to do something to get you into the house. We've been watching it and hell froze over in the meantime. Let's turn up the heat."

Tina became thoughtful and three pairs of eyes were on her. She smiled. "Why the hell didn't I think of this earlier?"

PREPARATIONS

WEDNESDAY, OCTOBER 24TH INTO THURSDAY, OCTOBER 25TH

TINA BORROWED three detectives from Fred Langley's agency. One to tail Lonnie Johnson. One to tail Marguerita Maria Guadalupe Delgado Espinoza. And one to watch the house on Nicollet Island. All of us were, by now, familiar faces to Lonnie and Margie. Hence the new faces. Tina met with Sheila Blomquist, Darren Youngblood, and Dennis Hopson, the three operatives Fred sent us, and explained what they needed to know to keep an eye on their respective charges.

Youngblood followed Lonnie to the county building at which he works and where he remained all day except for a sojourn to Jimmy Johns and back.

Sheila followed Margie twice to the grocery store and once to the hardware store. On Margie's fourth foray of the day, Sheila got caught at a light and lost her. But, thanks to our intel, picked her up again at the Nicollet Island house. She was there for about an hour. Two men unloaded the BMW of the stuff she'd presumably purchased at the grocery and hardware stores.

Hopson reported lots of activity at the house in the morning. But by noon, things had quieted down, only the orange BMW disturbing the afternoon. To relieve the boredom, twice he dirtied himself up and put on smelly and ragged clothes. The first time he knocked on the door, saying 'agua' and making drinking motions, he got chased away by some guy. The second time, an old woman took pity on him and gave him a bottle of water. He tried to play it for more and made eating motions, saying 'tamale', but she shooed him away with a lengthy string of Spanish. The only word he could make out was the oft repeated 'Diablo'.

We weren't idle. Tina spent the entire rainy afternoon in the garage painting a logo on the driver and passenger doors of the Flex. Gwen's bald head was bent with mine, trying to make badges that would pass for being official and not be seen for what they were: something created by amateur Photoshop jockeys. It took us all afternoon, but we did it.

Tina came in at six. She got reports from the Langley crew and told them to knock off at eight, unless there were fireworks, and be back on the job at five.

Tatty was at school and spent some time at the hospital. She arrived just after Tina came in.

There were plenty of leftovers, so I announced supper would be Hunter's Delight. Hunt for it and delight in it.

While we were eating, Tatty told us Logan was doing well, and they were moving him from ICU.

"Very good news," I said.

Tina had a pleased-with-herself look on her face. "We're one step closer to avenging his accident."

"What do you mean?" Tatty asked.

"I've devised a ruse I think will get us into that house," Tina said.

Tatty's face lit up. "You have?"

Tina nodded. "Yes. We're going to pretend we're gas company personnel tracking down a gas leak."

"Isn't that illegal?" Tatty asked.

"Very," I replied. "But Tina still thinks she's in the CIA at times and the ends justify the means."

The Boss waved her hand, I suppose hoping I'd vanish, and said, "It is illegal. Nevertheless, we have to get into that house and find out where they're holding those people."

Tatty looked at me, concern written all over her face, and then turned to Tina. "What if you get caught?"

"I'll probably lose my license." The tone in Tina's voice betrayed no concern of that ever happening.

"That means you can't be a detective?"

"That's what it means."

Gwen said, "We usually play by the books. We're honest and upright. Once in a while, we have to compromise on ethics. We might need to lie and even do something illegal, but that's very rare."

"I saw someone murdered," Tatty said in a quiet voice. "They are wicked. If this, what you plan to do, will stop them, then I don't see it as bad."

"I think we all agree with you, Tatty," I said. "But it is still illegal and technically we shouldn't be doing it."

"But why?"

"Because people have a right to feel secure in their homes and what we plan on doing violates that right. Of course, we think a greater right is at work here, but others might not agree. Those others primarily being lawyers and judges."

"But how can they not?" Tatty asked, clearly puzzled.

"Because even evil people have the right to privacy and the right to feel safe in their homes," I explained. "Rights apply to everyone or they apply to no one. Many a criminal has avoided punishment because the law enforcement folks violated some aspect of their rights."

"This seems wrong," Tatty said. "How can bad people have rights?"

"People have rights," I clarified, "not just good people. All people have certain inalienable rights. That is the basis of our legal system. If only some people have rights, what are those rights? Who determines what rights they have? And if they are given, can they be taken away? All important questions. In our system, the rights are theoretically granted by God to everyone. We are all equal."

"I guess it makes sense." Tatty's tone of voice indicated she still wasn't completely convinced. "Still, I hope you get these people and stop what they're doing."

"We're going to try, Tatty," Tina said, "we're going to try."

———

Thursday probably saw dawn and a sunrise, but the clouds and the rain and the snow prevented direct observation. However, since the day pretty much started out like any other day, it's safe to assume the sun was out there, somewhere, doing its thing like it has for the past few billion years. It's comforting some things don't change all that much.

I took the calls from Sheila, Darren, and Dennis informing us they were on duty at 5:07, 4:58, and 5:00, respectively. Lonnie left the house at six, walked to the bus stop, got on the bus, and rode downtown to work. Darren Youngblood followed in his car. A beige Buick, if I recall. Dennis Hopson reported all was quiet on the island. Sheila also reported things were quiet on Girard.

Breakfast preparations were well under way when Tatty came down to see if I needed any help, followed by Gwen ten minutes later. I told them they could keep me company. In spite of which, Tatty started cutting up an orange and Gwen began setting the dining room table.

"I have class today," Tatty announced, "and then I will go to hospital to see Logan."

"Give him my regards," I said. "I'll stop by as soon as I can."

She assured me she would tell him my message.

Tina came down a little before nine. Her hair was in a ponytail and she was wearing a gray shirt and black slacks. I think we were all staring. She saw us and said, "What?"

"You are not wearing your suit," Tatty said.

"I might have to do field work today," Tina replied. "Harry, see if David and Ed are available. Come to think of it, Stinky too."

"They might not be, at the last minute."

"I'll have to take my chances. Breakfast ready?"

She'd already used more words this morning before breakfast than she had in the previous month.

"Breakfast is ready. You all sit and I'll serve."

"I'll help, Harry," Tat said.

Breakfast passed in relative silence. When finished, I ran Tatty up to the U. Upon my return, I discovered Gwen had done the clean-up for me and was in the office with Tina. I called the boys. David and Ed were available. They'd been waiting for my call. Stinky, though, was engaged and not able to help us.

"David and Ed will be here within the hour," I told Tina.

"Good," she replied and continued her discussion with Gwen of the painting on the wall.

The painting (not the bright yellow one Mrs. Lowell had commented on, that one Tina had moved to a different room) is one of a series Tina did some years ago in the style of the American Impressionist painter Mary Cassatt. The title is

Autumn in the Country. I don't care for the painting all that much, but once a gallery was all excited at finding a "heretofore unknown work" of the artist. I took that to mean Tina had done good by Ms. Cassatt.

Around ten, the estrogen level in the house was lowered when David and Ed showed up. I told them the party was in the office. They went on in ahead of me and got seated. I followed and sat at my desk.

Tina began her spiel. "You are all aware of the sinister goings on below Nicollet Island. You are also aware how carefully our subjects have covered their tracks. I've decided the time has come to go out on a limb. We could all lose our licenses and be out of jobs if this backfires. If anyone, including you, Harry, does not want to be a part of this operation, there will be no hard feelings on my part. You are all friends and your leaving now won't change that."

She stopped, I assumed for our reactions, so I said, "In for a penny, in for a pound. Let's get these bastards."

Ed was the first to speak after me. "I have a wife and kids, but these people have to be stopped. I'm in."

"I'm in, Miss Wright," David said. "Like Harry said. Might as well see this through to the end."

"No need to ask me." Gwen had a wicked look on her face. "I have a couple baldies I need to make."

We all chuckled at Gwen's comment.

"Okay. Here's what we'll do," Tina began. "When we have the all clear from Fred Langley's people, we go over to the island house. We are gas company personnel checking for gas leaks due to reports we received of gas smells in the area. The Flex has a nice logo on the doors, and Harry and Gwen made up badges and ID. Once inside, we do two things: drop little bugs, I have five, and find the cave entrance, which will probably be in the basement. We need to be in and out in no more than fifteen minutes. Any questions?"

Ed asked, "How do we get past the dragon lady?"

"We have to impress on her — Diablo or no — this is an emergency. We'll push our way in, if we have to."

I held up my hand. "I looked up a crude translation of 'danger gas leak explosion'. It comes out as 'peligro explosión de fuegas de gas.' We can tell her that."

"Thanks, Harry," Tina said. "Any other questions?" No one had any. "I'll check on the situation after lunch and make the decision then to go today or not. Speaking of lunch, what do we have, Harry?"

"Not much. I can pick something up."

Gwen shook her head. "Not if you're going to the Castle."

David laughed. "Like Harry would go anywhere else?"

"What's wrong with the Castle?" Ed asked.

"Tell you what," Tina said. "Go get what you want and be back here by one and ready to roll."

"Do you have salad fixings?" Gwen asked.

"We do," I said.

"I'll stay here and make myself a salad," she replied.

"I'm going to the Castle," Ed said. "Anyone want anything?"

I gave Ed a slip of paper with my request on it and cash to pay for his and mine.

David said he was going to Byerly's deli. Tina asked him to pick her up something. I gave David cash to cover his and the Boss's lunches.

The guys took off. Gwen went to the kitchen, Tina stayed put, and I decided to keep Gwen company.

She smirked. "Don't trust me in your kitchen, eh?"

"Just here to help you find things and collect beverages."

"Yeah, right. That's okay, Harry. I wouldn't trust you in

mine, either. After all, you might sneak in some mini-hamburgers."

We laughed. I pointed out where things were when she asked and collected wine, beer, and water. The guys didn't take too long. David brought back two containers of pad thai and Ed brought back a Crave Case, slaw, and four large sacks of fries.

We dove into the food. David and Tina, opting for the Seyval Blanc, I chose Zin, Ed opened a Leinie, and Gwen drank water. Ed and I were still working on the Crave Case when Tina made the calls to Sheila, Darren, and Dennis. Sheila said Marguerita hadn't budged. Darren reported Lonnie was at work. Dennis said the rain and snow were keeping things quiet in the neighborhood.

"You guys are going to have to postpone demolition of that box of burgers. We need to roll now," Tina said.

Ed and I stuffed one last slider each into our mouths and got ready to go. Operation Center Point was on the move.

22

OPERATION CENTER POINT
THURSDAY AFTERNOON, OCTOBER 25TH

THE FLEX PULLED up across from the house on Nicollet Island, Gwen driving, at twenty-three minutes after one. We were a motley assortment of disguises and we weren't convinced we'd fool anybody. Tina rang the doorbell rather insistently. Finally, the old woman answered the door.

Tina began her spiel. "There have been gas leaks reported. We're checking all the houses to make sure we find the source. Your house is next."

The woman smiled and said, "No English."

Tina showed her the fake badge, pointed to the Flex with the gas company logo painted on the door, and said, "Peligro explosión de fuegas de gas."

The woman looked puzzled.

Tina repeated, "Explosión. Gas."

I took out my lighter and made explosion noises. While Tina indicated we needed to come inside. Finally the woman said, "Si," and a whole lot of Spanish we didn't understand, and let us come in.

We quickly went to work. Gwen remained in the Flex to be a pair of eyes on the outside situation. David took the upstairs, and Ed explored the main floor. Tina and I made our way to the basement. The space was crudely divided into several rooms. A laundry area; a bathroom; a couple bedrooms with mattresses and cots, which looked none too clean; and another room that had a desk, a couple of chairs, and a closet. Tina placed a bug under the desk and I placed one in one of the bedrooms. I was going through the desk and she was examining the closet when suddenly she said in Esperanto, "Rigardu tion! Falsa muro! Mi trovis la koridoro!"

She'd found a false wall in the closet and behind it a passage.

There was a hole in the floor and a ladder. We played our flashlights into the opening. It looked like the earth had given way and provided an entry point. I climbed down some fifteen feet and found myself in a tunnel, which was walled off from the main system under the island. One of those myriad side tunnels. There was another hole with another ladder. I peered over the edge, seeing what my flashlight might pick up. To my eye, I guessed the floor to be thirty feet down, ending in what looked to be a chamber in the bedrock.

I climbed back up. To Tina, I said, "I'd wager anything this leads to the big cave. This ladder goes to the old tunnel system, and there's another hole that goes into what looks to be bedrock and a room or tunnel."

"Unfortunately, we can't explore it now. But you are probably right. That's why this house is so important."

"Right."

"Okay. Let's go. We've been here too long already."

We put the fake wall back and headed upstairs. David and Ed were milling around. The look on the old woman's face indicated to me she was slowly coming to the realization we weren't with the gas company. We thanked her and told her all was well and left the house. Drizzle, snow, and freezing rain were turning the wintry day into a downright unpleasant night. We piled into the Flex and Gwen drove off. The old woman watching us from the door.

Gwen drove into the driveway and parked the Flex in the garage. Tina called Solstice, her renter of the former servants' quarters over the garages, and asked if she could paint over the gas company emblem. "We can't have that showing any longer," she said as we went into the house.

We followed Tina to the office and there we discussed what we found. David started us off. "Nothing much upstairs. I dropped a bug behind one of the beds. Just a couple bedrooms and a bath."

Ed was next, "There wasn't anything on the main floor either. I dropped a bug in the fake flowers on the coffee table. If I were to make a guess, I'd say the old woman lives there."

"From what I observed, I'd say the same," David said, "except they must get a lot of visitors. The one bedroom looked to be the old woman's, and the other was a well-provisioned guest room for a woman or man or maybe both."

"I think the basement is the scene of the action, or at least some of it," I said. "There are three rooms. Two serve as bedrooms and the third as some kind of office."

"And that's where I found the passage," Tina added. "Behind a false wall in a closet."

I described what I'd found. "I climbed down the first ladder and ended up in a walled off part of the old tunnel system. There was another hole which continued into a deeper cave. Unfortunately, I didn't have time to explore. But that deeper cave looks as though it could be part of the ancient system we entered from a different direction, following Logan's path."

"That's why the house is so important to them," Gwen said.

"Exactly," Tina replied. "The passage must lead to that large cavern where they hold the ceremonies. The participants enter and exit through the house."

"But where do they hold the victims?" Gwen asked.

"Probably, initially, in the basement," I said.

"Then they're probably transferred to an underground holding area," Tina added.

"So now what?" David asked.

Tina was hesitant. She doesn't like to give anything away. "I think we turn the information over to the police."

"They won't like how we got it," Ed said.

"No, they won't," Tina agreed. "But we don't have to tell them everything. We now have proof over seventy-five people are missing. There is the cave. The house and its connection to the tunnels and we're guessing the cave. We have three people who saw a ceremony being conducted that involved human sacrifice."

"Although the cave was clean and, as Cal pointed out, the observers had been smoking pot," I said.

Gwen chimed in, "That's going to be the rub. The judge sees they're smokin' and he'll chalk it up to psychedelic hallucinations."

"There's Tatty's hammer," I said. "The blood on it."

"But what does that prove?" David replied. "Nothing more than someone hit someone else with it. Doesn't mean seventy-five people were sacrificed to Aztec gods and goddesses."

"Did they run any tests on you, Gwen?" Tina asked.

"I was pretty much out of it," she replied. "I don't know."

"Are the police following up on the kidnapping?" David asked.

"There's no connection to our dynamic duo," Tina said. "They use agents to do their work for them. Nothing comes back to touch Lonnie or Margie."

Ed added, "And to be honest here, there are lots of illegal Mexicans in the Twin Cities. They'll do just about anything to not be deported. Especially if our subjects are taking care of them."

There was more, and it was more of the same. No sense in my boring you with it. We'd found what we were looking for. The problem now was we didn't seem to be able to do anything with the information.

The police weren't going to sit on Lonnie and Margie unless they had probable cause Lon and Marge had done something and, thus far, we couldn't prove anything. Those of us sitting there in Tina's office knew they had committed mass murder. We just couldn't prove it. That was the kicker.

And as sympathetic as Cal often was, he was in homicide and no murder — again, that we could prove — had been committed. He couldn't help us. Gwen had been taken and Gwen had been returned. And that's where we stood.

After Ed and David had gone home and Gwen had gone up to bed, Tina and I sat before the fire in the office while Tatty sat at my desk, studying. She'd reported Logan had been quite talkative and glad to see her. He'll be in the hospital until his parents can get their house ready to cater to the needs of an invalid. A bedridden invalid.

Tina was smoking a cigar and drinking Malmsey madeira. I was smoking my pipe and drinking port. "Where does all this leave us with the Lowells?" I asked.

"Their son was taken in by Brother Leonard and supposedly sent home by Brother Leonard. In truth, Edmund is already dead or waiting to die."

"We need to do something."

"I know. But this isn't the late eighteen hundreds and we aren't Pinkerton agents."

I thought about that comment. We'd conducted a frontal

assault so to speak on the house and gotten vital information. What if we did the same in the cave itself? To succeed, we'd need thin men and women who weren't too tall and preferably heavily armed in case they met resistance. Which seemed likely. I said the same to Tina.

"Interesting thought, Harry. See what you can find tomorrow. I did some reading on Aztec festivals. According to the Aztec calendar, this is a bloody month. Be very nice if we saved some lives."

23

SALMAGUNDI ARMY

FRIDAY, OCTOBER 26TH

THE BUGS WERE RELATIVELY quiet yesterday. Spanish. The old woman's voice and a man's.

Before Hopson knocked off for the night, he'd observed the arrival of Lonnie Johnson, which was confirmed by Youngblood. Lonnie had taken off in the van. Youngblood had lost him at a light but picked him up again at a homeless shelter, only to lose him again when a car pulled out in front of him and he had to slam on the brakes to avoid a collision. Hopson, though, reported the van's return at around nine at night. Lonnie and two men got out of the van and entered the house. A half hour later, Johnson left. Youngblood noted Johnson's arrival at home about twenty minutes later.

This morning, early, two bugs went silent. The one in the basement office picked up lots of talk. All of it in Spanish, except for a comment from the bedroom bug asking, "When do we eat?"

At five, Blomquist reported in and said the BMW wasn't in the garage. At quarter after five, there was quite a bit of talk going on being picked up by the bugs. The bug in one basement bedroom picked up chanting, around five-thirty, in a language that wasn't Spanish. And then the words I didn't want to hear: "Where are we going? I'm not going down there." The sounds of a scuffle and then silence.

The Aztec high priestess was gearing up for the weekend. I dropped Tatty off at school and agreed to pick her up at the hospital at four, unless all hell had broken loose. Back at home, Gwen was monitoring the bugs, which were going silent one by one.

"They've found us out, Harry," she said.

"Looks as though they have," I replied.

I called Sim's Security and asked if they had any thin, average height men or women, firearms handy, available today and through the weekend. Champagne (yes, that's what she said her name was) told me she'd check and get back to me.

I pictured the fissure in my mind and debated what equipment we could get through there. I thought we'd probably need sledgehammers, too. If I were in their shoes, I would have sealed the tunnels off again.

Pinkerton has a Twin Cities office, and I thought of giving them a call. However, when I found out they were no longer an American company, having been bought by a Swedish firm, I said to myself, no dice. There are plenty of domestic companies, no sense sending Lowell's money overseas.

The internet is a wonderful invention. So much more handy than the old yellow pages of my youth and early adult life. I looked up security firms in Minneapolis and Saint Paul. Much to my dismay, only Sims was local. At least that I could find. Now I had to get creative. I called Stinky. He answered on the third ring.

"Hey, Stinky. Harry Wright here."

"Hi, Harry. What can I do for you?"

"I need three or four guys. Girls would work too, who are

average height and thin and know how to use a firearm. Know anyone who might fit the bill?"

"You looking for a fight?"

"Protection in case I get into one and the possibility is high I will."

"I see. Let me think on it and I'll call you back."

"Talk to you later." I ended the call.

If Stinky rounds anyone up, they'll be used to a fight. The only problem will be their loyalty. And they wouldn't have a carry permit. So make that two problems.

Tina came down at nine. I'd made tea. But nothing else. Which probably wasn't much of a problem because Tina doesn't eat much for breakfast anyway. She sat in the dining room and I served her tea.

"Want toast? I'm kind of busy with work."

She raised her eyebrows, gave the question some thought, and finally nodded. I made her toast, gave it to her, and told her I was returning to the office. She joined Gwen and I twenty minutes later.

"You've been busy this morning," she said.

"Very," I replied and brought her up to date on what had happened.

She scrunched up her face, looking for all the world as though she were drinking lemon juice instead of tea, and said, "With Margie on the move this early, we can't take that as a good sign."

"No, we can't," I replied.

"And they've discovered they were bugged and are eliminating every one they find," Gwen added.

"The question is when," Tina said. "When do we move? Sooner rather than later, don't you think?"

"I do," I said.

"Me, too," Gwen added.

Tina was counting on her fingers. "Five of us."

Gwen interrupted, "Tina, I can't go through that fissure. I, I just can't. And I'm not sure you could. Physically. Nor Ed."

"Ed, I can see," Tina said. "He's a big guy. But I'm too large?"

"Well, um, your height, your hips, and your bust. Other than that, you'd do fine." Gwen had a smile on her face, and I was snickering.

"I see," she replied.

"For once, your imposing self is counterproductive," I said.

She glared at me.

"Just sayin'," I replied.

She sat back in her chair and closed her eyes.

The phone rang. I answered.

"Youngblood, here. Subject is leaving the address in his Toyota. I'm following. Instructions if I lose him?"

"Yeah. Check and see if he turns up at the house on Nicollet Island."

"Will do. Out."

Guy must've been in the army or still thinks he is. I announced, "Lonnie's on the move. My next paycheck says he's on his way to the island."

"Of course he is," Tina said. "There's only six days for them to sacrifice a whole lot of people, seeing we slowed them down."

Gwen shuddered. "Religion can be pretty stupid, but this is just downright gruesome and evil."

"We are going to do what we can to stop it," Tina said.

"What's your battle plan?" I asked.

"I'm thinking we launch a two-pronged assault. One through the tunnels and the other through the house."

"How are we going to go through the house?" Gwen asked.

"I don't think you want to know," I said.

"Whose side are you on, Harry Gill Wright?"

"Uh-oh. I'm in trouble now."

"Damn right you're in trouble." Then Tina smiled. "Harry is right, Gwen. You probably won't want to know. We're going to force our way in."

Gwen smiled. "Yeah, I kinda figured that one was coming."

The phone rang. I answered, "Wright Investigations."

"Mr. Wright? This is Champagne from Sim's Security. I have a man and a woman I can send over right away. I think they'll fit your requirements."

"Good. Send them on over."

"They're on their way."

I ended the call and announced, "Two on their way from Sim's."

"Did you call Three Sisters?" Tina asked.

"No, I didn't. How could I forget?"

"I don't know about you, Harry."

I got on the phone and in two rings got Melissa Olson. She's the older sister of Three Sisters.

"Hey, Harry. How can I help you?"

I explained what I needed.

"Kind of short notice, but I'll see if I can come up with someone."

I thanked her and hung up.

The phone rang, and I answered.

"Harry, this is Stinky. I found two brothers who'll work with you, but they want a thousand a day each. LeJohn and Abraham Washington. I'll be frank with you. They aren't much better than the people you're up against. I saved their lives. They're good for me. They'll be good for you because you're with me."

"They understand this might involve shooting?"

Stinky laughed. "Harry, LeJohn and Abraham wouldn't flinch staring down a hundred Taliban. Your subjects aren't going to scare them one bit."

"Okay. Send them over."

"They're on their way."

"Thanks, Stinky."

"You're welcome. Sorry, I can't join you but I'm on a case."

"Quite all right. Next time."

I relayed Stinky's information to Tina. She nodded.

Youngblood called and confirmed Johnson was at the house on the island.

A half-hour passed before Pho-dung Quang and Jenny Betts showed up from Sim's Security. I led them to the office and introduced them to Gwen and Tina.

"You are licensed to carry firearms?" Tina asked.

They answered they were.

"What I want you for is a search and rescue mission. There may be shooting. You will be party to trespassing and breaking and entering. Are you willing to break the law to save people?"

Jenny Betts said, no. Pho-dung wanted more information. Tina sent Ms. Betts away and explained in detail what we'd discovered to Pho-dung.

"You think people are alive and being held prisoner underground and this Marguerita woman is going to kill them and eat them?" Pho-dung summarized.

"Yes," Tina said.

"I will help you. But on my own. Not as an employee of Sim's. They would not approve of breaking the law."

"Welcome aboard Mr. Quang." Tina said.

The doorbell rang. I answered and let in LeJohn and Abraham Washington. I guessed both to be in their twenties. They were wearing black great coats and underneath them they were packing a considerable amount of heat. LeJohn had two 9mm pistols and a TEC-9. Abraham was carrying a 9mm pistol, a pistol-grip shotgun, and a MAC-10 with suppressor.

"Mr. Johnson said you needed help. We're here to help," LeJohn said.

"I see that," I replied. "Let me introduce you to the boss."

I guided them to the office and introduced LeJohn and Abraham to Tina, Gwen, and Pho-dung.

Abraham said, "We don't fear nobody and Mr. Johnson said you was good friends of his, sos we cuttin' you a deal. Ten Bens for each of us and we'll take down whoever you want."

Tina looked at them "Can you follow orders?"

LeJohn looked Tina up and down as though she was for sale and he was buying. "Depends whose givin' 'em."

"I am," she replied.

LeJohn looked at Abraham and said, "I don't know, Abie, I never taked no orders from a white ho befo."

"If you want your ten Bens, I suggest you not call me that again," Tina said.

Abraham said, "She's kinda uppity. I don't know LeJohn. Mebbe we don't want her money, in spite of what Mr. Johnson says."

Tina stood up. LeJohn stood a scrawny five-five and Abraham was an equally scrawny five-eight. Tina with her stiletto heels stood at six-three.

"She's one of them Amazons, Abie," LeJohn said.

Tina walked around her desk and stood facing the two men. "How many have you killed?" she asked.

LeJohn said, without hesitation, eight. Abraham took a little more time and finally decided on five.

"I've killed two with a rifle at a thousand yards. I killed another two with a poisoned knife. And I killed eleven with my bare hands. You two have a choice. You follow my orders or you go back out the way you came. What's it going to be?"

LeJohn said, "Mr. Johnson was right on, man. He said you had balls. He didn't tell us they was made of steel."

"You're like a goddamn, mother fuckin', female superman, you are," Abraham said and added a long drawn out and undulated, "shit," to emphasize his point.

"We'll follow your orders, Miss Wright," LeJohn said. "Mr. Johnson said you don't take no shit, but people can count on you. Where's our money?"

Tina went back to her desk. "You get paid when we're done with the job."

"Miss Wright, now how—"

"No argument. Mercenaries have no loyalty except to the dollar. If I give you your money now, your loyalty will be to your wallet. Not me. An intolerable situation. I keep the money till we're done. If you don't like it, Harry will show you out."

"We're your men, Miss Wright," LeJohn said. "Mr. Johnson says you're the best and if he says you're the best, well, you are."

Tina smiled. "Mr. Johnson is a good man. I have a lot of respect for him. He is the acme of faithfulness. You gentlemen have a seat."

LeJohn nudged Abraham and said, "You see, bro, we's already movin' up. Now we's gentlemen."

The doorbell rang. I checked who was there through the peephole. Helen and Heloise Olson from Three Sisters. I opened the door.

"Hi Harry!" They said in unison.

"Come on in, ladies." Helen and Heloise are identical twins. I believe they're in their late twenties. Their sister,

Melissa, is in her mid-thirties. All three have blond hair. They specialize in personal protection.

They followed me into the office. I made introductions.

"We volunteered to help you out because we didn't have anyone else available," Helen said. Or maybe Heloise said it.

Tina explained what we were facing. When she was done, Heloise (or maybe Helen) said, "You can count on us."

Abraham said in a loud whisper to LeJohn, "They ain't got no heat. Must gonna pretty face 'em to death."

Helen (or maybe Heloise) walked over to the brothers. "Stand up."

Abraham looked at LeJohn and a big grin appeared on his face. He stood, and it happened so fast I can't describe what happened. A flurry of arms and legs and Abraham was crumpled on the floor. In Helen's (or Heloise's) hands were the shotgun and the MAC-10.

"Now I'm packin' heat," she said.

LeJohn whistled and uttered a long drawn out, "shit."

The Olson twins sat down. Whichever twin she was said of the MAC-10, "This is really nice. Where'd you get it?"

LeJohn spoke. Abraham was beginning to uncrumple off the floor. "A guy we know in Chicago."

The doorbell rang. I got up, checked who was there and let in David and Ed. The gang was all here. I took them to the office and made the introductions.

Tina stood. "Now that everyone's here, we'll divide into teams. Gwen, Ed, and the Washington brothers will be with me. David, Pho-dung, and the twins will be with Harry. Gather around my desk." Tina took out from a drawer a map of Nicollet Island. "This is how we'll proceed."

Cal doesn't call her the General for nothing.

24

TWILIGHT OF THE GODS

FRIDAY AFTERNOON, OCTOBER 26TH INTO EARLY SATURDAY MORNING, OCTOBER 27TH

Clouds had blocked the sun all day. The temp never climbed out of the fifties and the wind chill made it feel a good ten degrees cooler. At two-thirty Tatty texted she was on the bus heading for the hospital. I texted back I'd meet her in Logan's room a little before four.

David and Ed left to pick up lunch for everybody. We'd all agreed on Wendy's. I also asked them to grab me a couple sledgehammers. While they were out, Hopson reported people were starting to show up at the house.

"Looks like they're gearing up for a party," I told Tina.

"I don't doubt there will be a lot of people there," she replied and, looking at the Washington brothers, added, "that's why we can't be trigger-happy. We're there to rescue the prisoners before they become shish kabob and get out."

Abraham was pouting. "She took my guns. I don't got nothin' to shoot up nobody."

Helen (but it may have been Heloise) said, "Come over here and get them. Besides, I left you your pistol."

LeJohn was yucking it up at his brother's expense, who just

sat there looking miserable. I have to admit the entire scene was worthy of a Guthrie Theater performance.

When David and Ed returned, I put the sledgehammers in my car and then joined the others in the dining room to eat. The burgers and fries were good. Not the Castle, but they passed.

After lunch, we retired to the office again. Wandering in behind us were Prudy, Isis, and Manly. We had a full house and all of their usual spots were taken. Isis jumped into Gwen's lap. I suppose she felt a certain kinship. Baldies of the world unite. Manly decided to sprawl out on Tina's desk. Prudy jumped up onto the sofa and sprawled out between LeJohn and Abraham.

"Impressive," Tina said. "You are now part of the family."

LeJohn didn't say anything. He just reached over and petted Prudy. Abraham said, "We ain't never been part of no family."

When someone makes a comment like that, there isn't anything of significance you can say in response.

A little before three-thirty, I took off for the hospital. By the time I got parked and up to Logan's room, the time was close to four. I said hello to Logan, Cynice, and Cindy. We exchanged pleasantries. I noticed Tat's backpack in a corner.

"Where's Tatty?" I asked.

"I'm wondering the same thing," Cynice said. "She went to the bathroom. What was it, ten, fifteen minutes ago?"

"I think so," Cindy said.

"Where's the bathroom?" I asked.

"I'll show you. Come on," Cynice said.

Down the hall and to the right to the public restroom. Cynice went in and came out.

"She's not there, Harry."

"Don't let it be," I said.

Cynice took in my face. "Oh, no. You don't think?"

"I do."

We fairly ran to the nurse's station, and I asked if they could page Tatiana Bogar. It was urgent. In a moment, I heard the page asking Tatiana Bogar to report to the nurses's station. We waited for a response, but none came. After about ten minutes, my phone chimed. I looked at the text message:

> You were told to stop. You said you would.
> Too bad you are liars. Hungarian for supper.
> Yum.

"They have her," I said. "I have to go."

I ran out of the hospital, got into my car, and drove like a maniac home. I left the car at the curb and ran into the house.

"They have Tatty," I yelled. "I'm going now. Who's coming?"

"Harry—"

"Not now, Tina. I'm getting Tatty."

"But, Harry—"

"No. You do what you want. I'm getting Tatty. Who's coming with me?"

David, Pho-dung, Helen, and Heloise chorused, "I am," and we ran to my car. Rush hour traffic slowed me down, but there was nothing I could do about it. We were on the island by five and prying up a manhole cover shortly after. We lowered ourselves, one by one, into the hole. At the bottom, standing in the warm, dry tunnel, I got my bearings and took off in the direction of the older tunnel and the caves. David and Pho-dung were carrying the sledge-hammers.

Behind me I heard Helen, or perhaps it was Heloise, say, "This is awesome. I never knew these even existed."

Pho-dung said, "Reminds me of stories my grandfather

told of living in tunnels fighting the French and the Americans. Not good. Not good at all."

I stopped. Before me was the side tunnel. Well, where the side tunnel was supposed to be. They had, as I suspected, bricked it back up. Pho-dung and I started going at it to knock the wall down. The sheet of pre-fab brick was pretty cheap, and we knocked a big enough hole in it for us to climb through in twenty minutes.

I entered first and sure enough, they'd blocked up where the tunnel had originally been sealed off. Pho-dung and I went at it again, and twenty minutes later had a hole we could crawl through. The smell of wet basement hit my nostrils.

"Steps up ahead," I said. "Be careful."

Down the steps we ran, and we entered the cave. I warned them about the hole up ahead. Behind me came oohs and aahs. The cave is beautiful. Hopefully, a day will come when I can just sit there and appreciate it. But that day wasn't it. We crossed the cave and traveled down the passage until we got to the narrow section.

I said, "This very narrow section is about seven feet long. You'll have to squeeze through. You will get wet. On the other side, it opens into a room. There's a crack in the wall which allows you to see into the large chamber. To the right is an entrance into the back of the chamber."

"Listen," Heloise (or maybe Helen) said. Drums and chanting sounded in the distance. It raised to a fever pitch and then silence. Then the chanting started up again.

"Oh, shit," I said.

"Let's not think about it and just get in there and stop it," David said.

"Right," I replied.

I didn't take my clothes off, but I did empty my pockets and took off my belt and put everything in a bag. I had a flashlight in my other hand. I squeezed in and sidled through. Helen and Heloise followed me, then Pho-dung, and finally David.

The main chamber of the cave was lit. I guessed the lights to be battery powered. The intensity was that of light at dusk. The stage area was around seven feet above the cave floor and much more brightly lit. There were, in addition to the electric lights, a couple of old fashioned torches. On the stage was an altar covered with blood, a skull rack, and a small hut. Behind the altar stood Marguerita. She wore a headdress of feathers and a blood-stained white robe. Her arms were covered in blood. She was chanting in what I guessed to be Nahuatl. At the base of the altar were two bodies. I saw flickering light and guessed a fire was burning on the cave floor. I could smell the odor of roasting flesh.

Pho-dung was carrying an H&K USP 40. David is not much of a gun person. He had his trusty 9mm Star Firestar. The twins weren't carrying any firearms, but had an array of stars, saps, and batons. I was carrying two thirty-eight caliber S&W Bodyguard revolvers and a monkey's fist slungshot.

"I'll go in first. Pho-dung, you follow me. Then David, Helen, and Heloise. I'll fire a warning shot to stop the proceedings, then we'll make our way to the stage. Let's go."

We came out at the back of the chamber on stage right. The crowd was in front of us, their attention riveted to the stage. The drums were beating. Marguerita was chanting. Two women were being brought on stage. They were undoubtedly the next sacrifices. They looked drugged. The second woman was Tatty. I fired my revolver at the ceiling and yelled, "Stop!"

The people near us were startled and backed away. But my shout and yelling stopped nothing. The first woman was stripped to her waist and laid on the altar. Four men held her arms and legs. Marguerita continued chanting and raised the knife in the air with both her hands. Pho-dung fired two shots from his forty caliber pistol and all of us screamed, "Stop!"

Marguerita said something in Spanish, and the crowd started to surge toward us. Her chanting continued.

"Quick. Form a buffer so I can get off a shot," I yelled.

David, Pho-dung, and the twins moved forward. I held my breath, aimed, exhaled half of it, slowly squeezed the trigger and the revolver fired. I missed Marguerita's hands and hit her headdress, sending several feathers flying. I fired the snub-nosed revolver again and once again missed.

Helen and Heloise had dropped several people, but had been pushed up against the wall. I saw Pho-dung pistol whip a monster of a guy and then fall under the weight of a group of women. David knocked down two. We were back to back now. I got out my slungshot and started swinging like a maniac. I felt it crunch a cheekbone, thwap the soft tissue of a neck, and thud into a skull. David was pulled away and buried beneath a pile of bodies.

A hand grabbed my shoulder, and I swung the slungshot and was rewarded with a scream. Hands were on my legs and I was losing my balance. A fist hit my cheekbone and stars exploded across my eyesight. I heard the word "Police" and a shot was fired. Something hit my head. There was a moment of intense pain and then nothing.

25

PUTTING HUMPTY TOGETHER AGAIN
SATURDAY, OCTOBER 27TH

THERE WAS no moon and there were no stars. There was no light. Only the blackness of night. There was no earth. There was nothing.

Yet something was shaking me. Was I wrong? Was there a God after all and He was shaking me awake? A woman's voice called my name. Huh. God is a woman. How novel.

I forced my eyes open. The shaking was too much. It hurt my head. Although my eyes were open, I didn't see anything, but the voice calling my name said, "Oh my God! He's alive!" The voice. I knew that voice. Tina? She was with me? But where was I?

"Harry! Can you hear me?"

I tried to speak, but nothin' doing. I closed my eyes and opened them. Everything was blurry, but I could see shapes. I tried raising my hand, but it didn't want to follow orders either.

A new shape joined the others. "We can take him next, Miss Wright." I was lifted up and set back down on something softer than what I had been on. Then I felt three or four things pull across me and they became tighter. From some place in my mind, the words "stretcher" and "straps" materialized. I had been put on a stretcher and strapped down. Then everything came flooding back to me. And only one person mattered. I tried to scream, but "Tatty" came out instead as a barely audible croak.

"What, Harry? What are you saying?" Tina's voice.

I tried again and merely croaked, "Tatty."

"She's okay, Harry. Tatty's okay."

The weight. The oppressive horror of my failure to stop Marguerita fell away. Tatty had not died. There is kindness and mercy in whatever is out there that is bigger than us and brought this place into existence.

I was lifted up, and I felt myself move. Tina's voice told me she was with me and wasn't going to leave me.

———

Strange dreams, or were they dreams, disturbed what I assumed to be my sleep. There was the one where Marguerita was a head with a giant mouth for a body. Her hands kept picking up people and dropping them into the mouth. Then she picked me up and let me go and I felt myself fall and fall and fall.

In another dream, I sat down to dinner, and there were Marguerita and Lonnie, and they kept telling me, "Try it. You'll like it." And then there was the one where I'm at the table and the cover was taken off the platter. Before me is Tatty, roasted, and with an apple in her mouth. I screamed. I screamed myself awake.

Tina was there saying, "It's only a dream, Harry. It's only a dream."

"Tatty."

"She's okay. Just sleeping off the dope they gave her."

"Oh God. I missed and I couldn't stop her."

"But she's okay, Harry. She's okay."

"Thank God. Thank God."

"It's okay, big brother. Lie down. You have a nasty wallop on your head and a nasty concussion to go with it. Just rest."

"Lowell. Edmund. Was he alive?"

"Yes. We found him alive. Now rest."

———

I opened my eyes. Tatty's head was using me for a pillow. The rest of her was in a chair next to the bed. I stroked her hair, and she woke.

"Hi, Harry."

"Hi, Tatty."

"Thanks for trying to rescue me."

"I'm sorry, Tatty."

"You have nothing to be sorry for. Not every Halloween Gambit is won."

"No, it's not."

"We would have died together. Instead, we are alive together."

"Yes, we are."

She intertwined her fingers with mine.

Tina spoke. "The hospital's going to release you two. You can rest at home better than here."

"What about the others?" I asked.

"David has a concussion, too. He's going home with Ed. Pho-dung was hurt rather badly and is staying in the hospital. Helen and Heloise are okay. Although Helen, or maybe Heloise, suffered a cracked rib. They're home. Melissa picked them up earlier. Gwen's fine. She's going to be staying with us a couple more days, then go home. LeJohn and Abraham were arrested and hauled off to jail. Cal took one look at them and that was it. Curtains. The MAC-10 didn't help their cause either. And I'm fine. Worried sick about you. But now that you're okay, I'm okay."

The doctor came in and gave me discharge instructions. Tat already had hers. Tina drove us home. Tat and I were in the back seat of the Flex. Gwen was in the front. Tat was sitting next to me. Her head on my shoulder. She whispered, "I'm so glad this is over."

"Me, too."

"Harry?"

"Yes, Tat?"

"I love you."

"I love you, too, Tatty."

She snuggled closer to me. That was the best ride home I've had in a very long time.

26

CAL'S RECAP

SUNDAY, OCTOBER 28TH

CAL CAME OVER AFTER LUNCH. I can't say I've ever seen him ecstatically happy. There's always a reserve. A holding back. A resignation to the fact he knows too much of the dark side of life to allow himself to let go and be one hundred percent happy.

"Good to see you up and about, Harry. You really gave the Red Baron a scare. I don't think I've ever seen her that shade of pale before."

"Might help if you had a heart, Swenson."

"I do, Buttercup. I just don't let it run the show."

"I see."

I interrupted their banter. "I still don't know what happened. I remember hearing someone yell 'Police' and then the lights went out."

Tina was at her desk. Cal was in the oversized wingback. Gwen, Tatty, and I were on the chesterfield.

Tina spoke. "After you left, I called Cal. I gave him what I had. Another kidnapping associated with the case we were investigating. Clear evidence harm was intended. Add to that all the other info and the judge issued a no-knock warrant to search the house and, most importantly, under the house to search for Tatty."

Cal continued, "Once we had that search warrant, it was pretty much my show. I got those two threats to humanity Stinky sent you arrested right away. Possessing illegal firearms and no concealed carry license. That's just for starters. Murder will get in there, eventually. Tina, Ed, and Gwen tagged along. Mostly to find you, Major, and your group. I think we might have to bust you all the way down to private. That was the most cockamamie plan I've seen you come up with yet. Jesus H. Christ. What the hell were you thinking?"

Tatty snickered, "The Halloween Gambit."

Cal was puzzled. "What the hell is that?"

"You have to play chess," I said.

"Oh. Anyway, with Tina along so we didn't waste time looking for that false panel, we busted into the house. Some-body started shooting. We had two officers down and they had two down. We stormed into the basement and Tina pointed out the panel. We started going down and they opened fire. Lost a good man. We dropped teargas grenades, put on our masks, and stormed the place."

"Where was the holding cell?" I asked.

"I'm getting there. It was down that second opening. A room off the tunnel. The guy you were looking for and ten others were in there, including two kids and two women. I left two men there. We continued on down the tunnel and came out into that cave. I yelled, 'Police!' and they started shooting at us. We shot back. It was wholesale pandemonium. People screaming and running everywhere. We had four officers down. They had two dead and five wounded, including Lonnie Johnson."

"And Marguerita?" I asked.

"She escaped."

I shook my head.

Cal continued, "We rounded up seventy-one people. We think a couple others might have escaped with Marguerita. Including the joker who was her high priest. An initial count puts the number of illegals at fifty-eight. We're still trying to sort out who was involved directly with the sacrifices and who was merely a worshipper. Although I think the whole lot of 'em should at least be charged with aiding and abetting. This has to be the most grisly thing I've run across in twenty-four years in the department."

"It's over," Tina said. "At least for us. The Lowells are flying in today to pick up Edmund. He's going to have one bad drug habit to get over. They've been giving him heroin to keep him passive. The others as well."

"I can see why people take it," Tatty said. "My God, the rush and euphoria, there is nothing like it."

"Yeah, that's another thing we can get them on. Heroin possession," Cal added.

"Oh, Ralph Lowell made our accounting a lot easier," Tina said. "He's writing us another check, this one for twenty thousand dollars. If that doesn't cover everything, we're to let him know. And if it does, the entire amount is ours to keep."

"Merry Christmas," I said. "I feel badly about the Washington brothers. They came here in good faith."

"Don't be, Harry," Cal said. "They're really bad people. Well, I'd best be going. I have lots to do. Paperwork's a killer. Catch y'all later."

Cal left, and Tina saw him to the door. She returned a few minutes later. Poured herself a glass of madeira and invited others, but got no takers. I would've, but no alcohol while recovering. She offered cigars to everyone. We refused. Gwen and Tatty even relocated to the living room.

Tina lit the cigar and blew smoke towards the ceiling. She

raised her glass. "To another case brought to a successful conclusion."

"Here, here," I said.

She drank madeira. "I was scared, Harry. I don't know what I'd do if you weren't here."

"You got along just fine before I moved in."

"I did. But that was then, and this is now."

"Well, I'm alive. In spite of myself. And I'm here. With you."

"I'm glad, Harry. Very, very glad."

27

EPILOGUE

TATTY WENT HOME to her family in Hungary for Christmas. The semester ended December 20th, and she flew out on the 21st. We exchanged emails, and I called her on Christmas Day to wish her a merry Christmas. But after Christmas she disappeared, and I didn't hear from her. I sent a few emails, but no answer.

On New Year's Eve, a little after five in the afternoon, my phone rang. The call was from Tatty.

"Hi, Tatty."

"Happy New Year, Harry."

"Same to you from me in seven hours."

She giggled and then her tone got sober, although I suspected she wasn't. "Harry, I wanted to tell you I'm not coming back for Spring Semester."

"Okay. I'm sorry to hear that. May I ask why?"

"Yes. You see, uh, um, well, I'm really sorry, Harry, but I love him and—"

"You and Lazlo are getting married?"

There was silence and finally, "Yes, we are going to get

married. I'm going to go to university in Budapest. I'm sorry, Harry. Please don't be mad at me."

There it was. What we both knew would eventually happen. And now it was happening. "Tatty, I'm not angry. I'm happy for you. We both knew this would happen eventually—"

She was crying. Alcohol sensitized emotions. "But I love you, too, and what we had was so very different and…"

When she didn't continue, I said, "Tatty, I'm very happy for you and Lazlo. I truly wish you the best. When's the wedding?"

"In the spring."

"Let me know the date and I'll try to make it."

"You will?"

"I'll try."

"Harry. I wish. I hoped—"

"Tatty, you're going to be very happy. And I'm happy for you."

"Thank you. My most wonderful friend. And our next game… How do you Americans say it? I'm going to whup your ass? Is that right?"

I laughed. "Yes. We say that. Goodbye, Tatty. I wish you the best, my friend."

"Goodbye, Harry. You are in my heart, always."

The call ended and so did that phase of my life. I wiped a tear, took a deep breath, and got a cup of tea.

In the next tournament where we found ourselves matched against each other, she did indeed whup my ass. I'm glad things are back to normal.

AFTERWORD

I hope you enjoyed *Festival of Death*.

If you did, please leave a review where you bought the book and on your favorite social media sites. Your review is like word of mouth advertising. And it is pure gold.

Enter my World

Enter my world and you'll find mysteries were never so good. Just click or tap the link below.

There's nothing like a good slow burn mystery. The quirky characters. The eccentric sleuth. The bumbling police detectives. The nefarious villain. And of course, the leisurely pacing until we reach the thrilling climax.

If you are new to the Justinia Wright Private Investigator Mysteries series, then *Festival of Death* is an excellent entry point into the series and into my world.

Tina and Harry are an homage to Nero Wolfe and Archie Goodwin. I so loved Rex Stout's world that I wanted to create one in the same style, but set in Minneapolis and the present day.

In my series, you'll discover the same type of exciting

stories, eccentric and quirky characters, and wicked killers as Stout wrote about years ago.

So just click, tap, or scan the QR code below to enter my world of mystery and mayhem. You will get a free copy of *Vampire House and Other Early Cases of Justinia Wright, PI* and you'll get my monthly email containing news and curated content. The game is afoot!

Yes, I want to enter the world of Tina and Harry Wright!

BOOKS BY CW HAWES

CW is a multi-genre author. The books below are portals to his many exciting worlds. And no AI was used in the writing of these books.

Justinia Wright Private Investigator Mysteries

Justinia Wright is the PI with panache. These slow burn mysteries, written in homage to Rex Stout's Nero Wolfe, are sure to satisfy your craving for intriguing puzzles, quirky characters, and wise-cracking humor.

Vampire House and Other Early Cases of Justinia Wright, PI
Festival of Death
Trio in Death-Sharp Minor
But Jesus Never Wept
The Conspiracy Game
A Nest of Spies
When Friends Must Die
Death Makes a House Call
To Right a Wrong
The Nine Deadly Dolls

Ripples on the Pond
Christmas with the Wrights
Minneapolis's Finest
Jack in the Box
Sauerkraut Days
Justinia Wright Private Investigator Omnibus Edition

Magnolia Bluff Crime Chronicles

Tense slow burn mysteries set in our favorite town in the Texas Hill Country.

Death Wears a Crimson Hat
Ten Million Ways to Die
Who Mourns Elektra?
Death by Moonlight

Pierce Mostyn Paranormal Investigations

The X-Files meets Cthulhu. Pierce Mostyn does battle with inter-dimensional monsters bent on the destruction of humanity.

Nightmare in Agate Bay
Stairway to Hell
Terror in the Shadows
Van Dyne's Vampires
The Medusa Ritual
Demons in the Dunes
Van Dyne's Zuvembies
In the Shadow of the Mountains of Madness

The Rocheport Saga

A post-apocalyptic adventure series in the style of cozy catastrophes such as *Earth Abides* and *Day of the Triffids*. Join Bill Arthur as he strives to build a new and better world on the ashes of the old.

The Morning Star
The Shining City
The Divided City
The Troubled City
By Leaps and Bounds
Freedom's Freehold
Take to the Sky

Decopunk

Alternative history adventures in a world where World War II never happened and swing is still king.

From the Files of Lady Dru Drummond
The Moscow Affair
The Golden Fleece Affair

Rand Hart Adventures
Rand Hart and the Pajama Putsch

Tales of the Macabre

For the horror lover in you.
Do One Thing For Me
Metamorphosis
What the Next Day Brings
Ancient History

Anthologies

Enjoy CW's stories in these short story collections.

The Phantom Games
Beyond the Sea
Overmorrow
Arachnapocalypse! The Anthology
Once Upon a WolfPack

You can find all of CW's books at Amazon. Just click, tap, or scan the QR code.

ABOUT THE AUTHOR

CW Hawes has written over 50 novels and shorter works of fiction, and is the impetus behind the very successful multi-author series Magnolia Bluff Crime Chronicles, produced by the Underground Authors. He was also a successful poet and had over 200 poems appear in ezines and and print.

After 35 years of working in county government, he retired at the beginning of 2015 and began a second career as a fiction-eer. Perhaps some of Justinia Wright's attitude towards government can be traced to her creator's own experiences. Perhaps.

CW lives in Southern California with family. He enjoys reading, writing, chess and other board games, his daily morning walk, and contemplating the meaning of life while smoking his pipe. He also hasn't met a doughnut or a pizza he doesn't like, is something of a tea snob, and rocks out to Handel and Vaughan Williams.

You can get curated content and the occasional free story when you join his mailing list, and you can reach him at his website, on X, and also Facebook. Just click, tap, or scan the QR codes.

Mailing List:

Website:

X (Twitter):

Facebook: